INVISIBLE INKLING

THE WHOOPIE PIE WAR

INVISIBLE INKLING

THE WHOOPIE PIE WAR

EMILY JENKINS

ILLUSTRATIONS BY HARRY BLISS

BALZER + BRAY
An Imprint of HarperCollins*Publishers*

For my family—E.J.
For Tate Stephen Charuk—H.B.

Balzer + Bray is an imprint of HarperCollins Publishers.

Invisible Inkling: The Whoopie Pie War
Text copyright © 2013 by Emily Jenkins
Illustrations copyright © 2013 by Harry Bliss

Library of Congress Cataloging-in-Publication Data
Jenkins, Emily, date.
The whoopie pie war / Emily Jenkins ; illustrations by Harry Bliss. — 1st ed.
    p.   cm. — (Invisible Inkling ; [#3])
Summary: "Hank Wolowitz and Inkling, his invisible bandapat friend, try to
save the family ice-cream store's business from a whoopie pie food truck parked
outside." — Provided by publisher.
    ISBN 978-0-06-180226-3 (hardcover bdgs : alk. paper)
    [1. Imaginary playmates—Fiction.   2. Imaginary creatures—Fiction.   3. Ice
cream parlors—Fiction.   4. Ice cream trucks—Fiction.   5. Family life—New York
(State)—New York—Fiction.   6. Brooklyn (New York, N.Y.)—Fiction.]   I. Bliss,
Harry, date, ill.   II. Title.
PZ7.J4134Who 2013   2012030493
[Fic]—dc23

Typography by Erin Fitzsimmons
13 14 15 16 17   CG/RRDH   10 9 8 7 6 5 4 3 2 1

First Edition

Contents

I Asked if We Could Get
a Black Mamba

Hey there.

By now, you know all about Inkling. You know he's an invisible bandapat. You know he speaks English, Yiddish, and Mandarin. You know he sleeps in my laundry basket. You know he came to live with me in September of fourth grade when I rescued him from Rootbeer, the hungry French bulldog who lives across the hall.

You know that bandapats are an endangered species from the Peruvian Woods of Mystery. Or possibly the redwoods of Cameroon. Or the Canadian underbrushlands.

Inkling never gets his stories straight. In fact, he's a liar. He lies so often, I sometimes suspect he's a secret agent. Who else would have that much to hide?

Nobody I can think of.

Though a secret agent would probably lie **better** than Inkling does.

Hopefully you also remember that we've got to keep hush-hush about Inkling living with me. I can't tell my parents, my sister Nadia, or my friend Chin from downstairs. Scientists are looking for the last of the bandapats. They want to trap them and take them to top-secret labs. They want to know what makes the bandapats invisible. They wonder why the bandapats can only be seen in mirrors and whether eating so much squash has anything to do with it.

The other reason Inkling has to stay hush-hush is that Mom won't let me have a pet. She says Dad, Nadia, me, and seven hundred books—that's already more than she can handle in a small apartment.

She's really serious about the no-pet thing. Last year before Inkling came, I asked if I could get a black mamba. Sure, they're lethal, but people keep poisonous snakes as pets all the time. Black mambas grow fourteen feet long. They're the fastest snakes in the world. Their heads are shaped like coffins. Even the insides of their mouths are black. Once, one was found with a full-grown parrot in its belly.

I read about them in my venomous-reptiles book. They're for-serious one of the coolest snakes alive.

Mom said no.

Then I asked for a rattlesnake. It would be a lot smaller than a mamba.

Still no.

Then I asked for a hedgehog.

No.

"Just a bitty hedgehog," I said. "A pygmy one." Pygmy hedgehogs are tiny, and you can feed them cat food. Or mealworms. Or vegetables. Nadia showed me stuff about them on the internet.

Mom sighed.

I told her they're only the size of an egg and they just need a rabbit hutch to live in.

"No!" Mom barked.

All right, then.

When Mom starts barking, it's time to stop asking.

You see, there's no way she'd say yes to Inkling. He is

much bigger than a pygmy hedgehog, and he eats a lot more than a rattlesnake.

That's why I'm asking you: please, please, **please**, promise not to say anything to anyone after you're done reading this. It's like a classified document.

From
Hank Wolowitz

LISTEN UP!
INKLING IS NOT A PET.
N-O-T NOT.
THE IDEA OF HIM BEING A PET IS AN INSULT TO HIS DIGNITY.
IN FACT, INKLING IS THE BEST FRIEND A BOY COULD EVER HAVE. HE SWIMS A RECORD-BREAKING BACKSTROKE. HE HAS TRAVELED FROM THE VOLCANOES OF INDONESIA TO THE DESERTS OF NORWAY.
WHAT ELSE? HE IS EXTREMELY WITTY, BRAVE, CUTE—AND YET SENSITIVE TO THE FEELINGS OF OTHERS. ALSO, AN EXCELLENT MONOPOLY PLAYER.

INKLING IS NOT A LIAR.
HE IS NOT A SECRET AGENT.
HE IS ALSO REALLY, REALLY NOT A PET.

Sorry.
Inkling wrote that when I left my room for a minute.

They All Taste Like Baby Food

I totally need to get hold of some canned pumpkin. I am going to hijack some when Dad's not looking. I've got a Ziploc bag in my pocket.

Pumpkin is Inkling's favorite food. Now that Halloween is over, it's been hard to find. I don't know if he'll like canned, though. Canned pumpkin is precooked and mashed. Bandapats like their squash raw. Still, it's worth a try, right? This morning, Dad is trying out pumpkin-ice-cream recipes down in the kitchen of our family's ice-cream shop, Big Round Pumpkin: Ice Cream for a Happy World.

Did you know that despite the name Big Round Pumpkin, our shop has never sold pumpkin ice cream?

Dad has tried and tried to make some. It always comes out gross.

Now, it's close to Thanksgiving. Brooklyn food shops are making pumpkin pies, pecan squares, apple dumplings. Time to try again.

I promised Inkling I'd snag some leftover canned pumpkin for him to taste. But so far this morning, I've missed every chance. Probably because Joe Patne is here, helping us cook.

Patne makes me nervous.

A thing about Patne is, he used to be my friend. He's come to my birthday parties and I've been to his. He was on my owl-pellet team at Science Fellow summer camp. Then he started going to after-school programs every day. I hardly ever saw him anymore. Now he's friends with this guy Henry Kim, who treats me like some tagalong kindergartner.

My best friend, Wainscotting, moved away just before fourth grade started. Without him, I'm not exactly Lord Popular. I do have Sasha Chin from downstairs. She and I built the Great Wall of China out of matchsticks together. Now we're working on the Taj Mahal. But aside from Chin, I don't have any other *visible* friends.

My dad invited Patne over without even asking me.

Here in the ice-cream-shop kitchen, we made a custard ice-cream base. Now three pots of canned pumpkin are cooking: one with vanilla, cream cheese, and honey; one with nutmeg and cinnamon; one with melted chocolate. The shop doesn't open till noon, so there are no customers yet. Dad stirs the pots with wooden spoons. Patne and I eat orange sprinkles from small plastic dishes.

The nearly empty cans of pumpkin are sitting on the counter. Calling me.

But Dad is always here. Stirring. Making jokes. Watching.

Finally, the phone rings and Dad takes himself out to the front of the store to talk. I have to get this pumpkin for Inkling. Barefaced in front of Patne, there's no other way. I grab a spatula and scrape the leftover pumpkin from the cans into my Ziploc.

"Why are you doing that?" Patne asks.

I have a lie prepared. I lie a lot now that Inkling lives with me. I feel bad about it—but what else can I do? "I'm gonna drop it out the fourth-floor window later," I tell Patne. "See it splat."

"Cool," he says, lighting up. "I did that with applesauce once. But we only live on the second floor, so I didn't get a really good splat."

I picture it. "Another problem is, applesauce is tan."

Patne nods. "You couldn't see it on the pavement that well."

"That's why I think the pumpkin will be good," I say. "Nice and orange. Chocolate pudding could work, too."

"I'd rather eat the pudding," Patne says. "Pumpkin's good because you don't want to eat it, and your dad's not using those leftovers. So it isn't a waste."

"True," I say. For a moment I've forgotten about Inkling and how he's waiting for the canned pumpkin. It seems like I really *am* going to splat it—until Patne says:

"Can I come upstairs with you? Help with the splat?"

"No!" I blurt.

"Aw, come on. I won't actually drop it. You can do that. I'll just be there as a witness."

"Not a good idea."

"Why not?"

I can't tell him I was lying about splatting the

pumpkin. I can't tell him I need to feed it to my invisible bandapat, who's had to settle for cheap acorn squash since the last of the Halloween jack-o'-lanterns hit the trash. Can I?

No.

I have to make sure Patne doesn't come upstairs. I have to make sure we don't splat the pumpkin. I can't let Inkling down.

Except: Patne is acting like he thinks I'm a person with good ideas. Like he wants to hang around with me, for once.

He doesn't always act this way.

"Okay," I tell him. "We can splat it together. There's a good spot out my sister Nadia's bedroom window."

Dad comes back. The three of us taste the pumpkin mixtures that have been cooking on the stove.

Hm.

Meh.

Yuck.

They all taste like baby food.

Dad thinks the cream cheese–honey-vanilla one might turn out okay once it's mixed with the custard, and sets that one in the fridge to chill. "But okay isn't

really good enough," he says. "I'll try again tomorrow."

"Why not just skip pumpkin ice cream?" asks Patne. "Why not stick with regular flavors?"

"Ice-cream shops do great in the hot weather," Dad explains as he sets up the big machine to churn a batch of espresso double shot that's been chilling. "Once it gets cold out, we have trouble finding customers. Making flavors for the winter holidays really helps. People will come in for pumpkin at Thanksgiving or candy cane at Christmas."

"Or latke-and-applesauce at Hanukkah," I add. "We should make that, Dad."

"I already told you no on that one, Hank," Dad reminds me.

I remember. But I still think we should do a Hanukkah ice cream. I have lots of ideas written down in my flavor notebook. I just haven't invented one good enough, yet. Maybe noodle kugel? Or creamed herring?

Okay, probably not creamed herring.

"Also," Dad goes on explaining to Patne, "a lot of our business is selling ice cream to restaurants for seasonal desserts. If I can tell them I have pumpkin ice cream, not just vanilla, they'll buy a lot. They'll put it on pecan pie or other holiday treats they have planned. I need to make flavors that other ice-cream companies don't have."

"Big Round Pumpkin ice cream is at fifteen restaurants," I tell Patne.

Dad coughs. "Only twelve now, actually."

Oh.

I am pretty sure it was fifteen before.

"Two of them started making their own," says Dad. "And one of them switched to a cheaper vendor."

"Is that bad?" asks Patne.

"Let's just say, I hope it's not a trend," says Dad. And he laughs—but he doesn't sound happy.

Which Is More Fun,
Alien Poo or Science?

D̲ad gives us an early lunch in the shop. Then my sister, Nadia, arrives for work, all sharp elbows and spiky hair. She barely talks to us as she ties on her apron and texts her boyfriend, Max. She and Dad open for customers. My job is dealing with garbage and recycling, but I can't do that until late in the day. Dad sends me home to play.

Patne and I run the half block back to my family's apartment. I am careful not to let the bag of pumpkin break open in my backpack.

Upstairs, Inkling's nowhere I can find him. I check

for movement by the plants. I feel in the laundry basket. I look for indentations in the couch pillows. Nothing.

I'd be surprised if he's out. He doesn't like to go by himself much. People step on his tail. Dogs try to eat him.

More likely he's asleep on top of the kitchen cabinets. There's a heating vent up there.

Mom's busy on her laptop. Patne and I sneak into Nadia's room with our bag of pumpkin.

Back when she was eight, Nadia asked to have her room painted pink. It's still pink, but now she's got a gray wool blanket on her white princess bed. There are stacks of books and boxes of art supplies all over the floor.

I haven't been in Nadia's room for ages. She's always yelling at me for going in there and messing with her stuff, only it isn't me. It's Inkling. On Nadia's dresser is a stash of hair products. When the apartment is empty, Inkling likes to fluff up his fur with them and admire himself in the mirror.

Patne and I lean out the window. The sidewalk, four flights below, is damp from this morning's drizzle. A perfect dark gray.

Patne has the Ziploc and is squeezing the pumpkin back and forth inside it. "There's something gross about this," he says. "I can't believe we ate some earlier."

"We didn't *like* eating it."

"Yeah, but right now it doesn't even seem like a food. It seems like . . ."

"Alien poo," I say.

"Yes!"

"Actually, Martian poo." I say. "'Cause Mars is the orange planet, and all the Martian plants are orange. Eating them makes the Martian poo orange!"

"Actually Mars is the *red* planet," Patne corrects.

Oh. "Well, Jupiter, then," I suggest.

"There's no evidence of life on Jupiter," Patne says. "The whole planet is made of gas."

"Who cares about evidence?" I yell. "We have a Ziploc full of alien poo to drop on the sidewalk. The question is not, Where's the evidence? The question is, Which is more fun, alien poo or science?"

Patne doesn't answer.

A thing about me is, I have an overbusy imagination. People complain about it a lot. Especially people like teachers and parents; people who like facts, and paying attention, and cleaning my room when I say I will.

Maybe people like Patne, too. He's looking at the floor like he doesn't know what to do.

I did just yell at him.

I know I should probably say sorry. I know I definitely should. But I can't say sorry when I'm confused about what I'm sorry for. Like is it, "Sorry I forgot that Mars is red and Jupiter is gas when I know outer space stuff is really important to you?" Or is it, "Sorry I yelled?" Or is it, "Sorry I acted like I knew what was important and you didn't?"

If I'm being honest, I actually want Patne to say sorry to *me*. "Sorry I took all the fun out of your alien-poo idea. Sorry I made you feel like you weren't sciencey enough to be my friend."

But that's not gonna happen, so I jump up and down, point out the window, and yell, *"Splat splat splat!"*

Patne leans out. He launches the Ziploc onto the sidewalk.

"Splat!" he yells.

The bag bursts. Orange mush sprays out across the sidewalk like an explosion—

—and all across Seth Mnookin, my neighbor.

We Thought It Would
Make a Good Splat

Mnookin is wearing a suit. I have never seen him in a suit. Usually he looks like he just got up from a nap.

Now his suit is covered in pumpkin up to the knees.

His dog is, too. Rootbeer is barking and jumping at us, as if she could bite four stories up.

"Is that you, Nadia?" Mnookin calls, shading his eyes.

"No, sir. It's Hank, sir," I say.

"Did you just throw—oh, heck, what is that—did you just throw orange paint at me?" Mnookin asks.

"It's only cooked pumpkin. I'm really sorry. My friend

Patne is sorry too."

"This is my only suit, Hank." Mnookin sounds upset. "I have to be at a funeral in an hour."

"I didn't throw it on purpose," I say. "My friend Patne didn't throw it on purpose, either. It just slipped out of our hands."

"I don't have another suit," Mnookin repeats, in a daze.

Suddenly, a hand grips the back of my shirt. Mom. "What's going on, boys?"

"Our hands slipped," I say. "Mnookin's suit got splashed by accident."

"What?" She leans out the window. "Seth! Are you okay?" She turns on me. "What's on him, Hank? What did you throw?"

"Canned pumpkin." I can't look her in the eye.

"Come up to the apartment, Seth," Mom calls down. "I can clean your suit if it's only pumpkin. It shouldn't stain." Then she turns to me and Patne. "I will talk to you boys *later.*"

Mnookin and Rootbeer come up. Mom wipes the suit with a damp rag and a little dish soap. She makes me and Patne rinse Rootbeer in the tub, which is a lot

harder than you'd think. The dog scrabbles so we can't rinse her back feet. Then she runs away and won't let us dry her. She leaves wet footprints in the kitchen as she snarfles around looking for scraps of food.

Mom gives us a bucket and scrub brush. We have to clean the sidewalk, too. "Sorry my mom is so cranky," I say to Patne as we pour water on the cement.

"My mom is cranky, too," he says. "Maybe even more than yours."

I'm grateful to him for saying that.

After Patne goes home and Mnookin heads off, Mom sits me down on the couch. "Anything you want to say to me about what happened today?"

Sheesh. Why do grown-ups always ask that? Of course there's not anything I want to say. I never want to talk about it again. I was hoping she'd forgotten about it by now.

I look at my thumbs.

"Hank, I asked if there was anything you want to say," Mom prompts.

"Do you think we'll ever make a good pumpkin ice cream?" I ask her. "The flavors we made with Dad came out gross. And do you know why there are no orange ice-cream flavors? Is it the color? Because back when I was trying to invent Halloween flavors in my flavor notebook, I realized: there's no orange ice cream. Orange sherbet doesn't count. It's a flavor from the olden days. Maybe no one liked it even then. Except! Listen to this! I bet *Martians* would like orange sherbet. Did you know Mars isn't called orange even though it looks orange? It's 'the red planet.' But when you look at pictures of Mars, it for-serious looks orange, so I think their food is probably orange, too. Only of course, since they're Martians they wouldn't *call* it orange 'cause their whole world is orange. To them it's just normal. Also, they don't speak English."

"Hank!" Mom is shouting now.

"What?"

"Why did you throw canned pumpkin out the window?"

Oh.

That's what she wanted me to talk about.

"We thought it would make a good splat," I say, my voice small.

"You admit you dropped it on purpose."

"Kind of."

"You planned ahead, then. You went into Nadia's room to get a good spot over the street."

"Kind of."

"You did."

"Yes."

"Earlier, you said your hands slipped. That was not the truth."

"Right."

"You can't drop things out the window!" yells Mom. "We are pacifists!"

My parents being pacifists means I'm not allowed to play Grand Theft Auto, watch *South Park*, or learn martial arts. It also means they always want me to find a peaceable solution to my problems. And not drop stuff out the window. "Kill them with kindness" is Mom's new favorite phrase. She means, defeat your enemy by being a kinder, better person than he is.

"You can't lie to me!" Mom is still yelling. "What on earth were you thinking, Hank?"

I was thinking about making Patne like me, I guess. I can't make myself say that out loud.

The Technical Term
Is Floppy Bits

While Mom is yelling, I let my brain do something else. I'm thinking, Maybe I can make some bathrooms for my Lego airport. They could be red. I've used most of the gray, brown, black, and white bricks, so I have to use a bright color. Red walls could look good with orange sinks, maybe.

I head into my room as soon as she's done with me. From under the bed, I drag out the airport. Then I pat inside my laundry basket for Inkling. "Wake up!" I say when my hand connects with his soft ears.

"I'm awake." The clothes shift around.

Pruhtutututututut. Inkling shakes himself like a dog. It's a thing he does when he's first getting up.

"You want to build our airport bathrooms red?" I ask. "With orange sinks?"

"No."

"Why not?"

"Because I don't."

"Why not?"

"I said I don't."

"Okay, fine. Do you want to do them yellow? We have almost as many yellow pieces as red."

"No."

"Green?"

"No."

"Orange?"

"I don't want to do the airport bathrooms at all," Inkling snaps.

"How will people use the bathroom, then?"

"You splatted my pumpkin!" he yells.

Huh? Oh yeah. "I'm sorry."

"That was my lunch."

"I know, I just—"

"You tell me you'll bring me canned pumpkin. I wait

all morning for it. Finally, I get tired of waiting. I go into Nadia's room to fix my fur. I'm only in there a couple minutes when you come in with that guy who isn't even nice to you."

"Joe Patne."

"Joe Patne, right. And it's not like he's even funny or anything, but you give him my pumpkin!"

"He is too funny," I say.

"Maybe," says Inkling. "Maybe he's funny, but he's not nice. Anyway, Patne didn't even eat the pumpkin. You guys just splatted it. Like it wasn't important to anyone. I'd been waiting for it all morning."

"I'm sorry."

"You know what, Wolowitz? Think before you act. Before you go splatting someone's special treat across the pavement."

I don't know what to say.

I did splat his treat across the pavement.

I did.

"Come on," I say. "Can't we just forget it and work on the airport?"

"I have problems, Wolowitz," Inkling says. "Problems you wouldn't understand. Problems that would have seemed a lot better with a belly full of pumpkin."

"What problems?"

"Personal ones." The laundry basket tips over, and Inkling bounds out.

"What personal ones?" I call.

His voice is coming from the top of my dresser now. "You're not going to understand, and you can't help."

"Try me."

"Well, I have a very nurturing spirit," Inkling says. "I'm sure you've noticed."

"Okay."

"And I'm nine. In bandapat years that's a grown-up."

"I know."

There is a pause. Finally, Inkling yells: "I WANT A CUTIE BANDAPAT CUB THAT WILL EAT CHEWED-UP FOOD OUT OF MY MOUTH!"

"*Eeeewwww!*" I had no idea he was going to say that.

"Don't say *ew*!" snaps Inkling. "You remember how emperor penguin dads hide penguin babies under their belly flaps?"

"Yeah."

"Is that *ew*?"

"No. That's cool, actually." The penguin dads keep

the pengies warm for months while the moms are out foraging. I read about it in my *Creatures of Antarctica* pop-up book.

"So, bandapat males have—well, the technical term is *floppy bits*. We have floppy bits on our undersides, and—"

"On your bellies?"

"Yes. The cubs hang out there in the cold weather. It gets very cold in the Ukrainian glaciers."

"Is it a pouch?"

"No!" Inkling sounds exasperated. "I told you, it's floppy bits. Anyway," he continues, "I haven't seen any other bandapats since our homeland in the volcanoes of Indonesia was destroyed by scientists. I have no one to bandapat around with. If I only had a cub, Wolowitz, I'd teach it everything."

"Like what?"

"Like how to drop on enemies from high branches, and how to eat pumpkin without getting strings in its teeth. I'd show it how to backstroke and catch Oatie Puffs in midair."

"You can show me how to catch Oatie Puffs if you want," I offer.

"You're missing the point!" Inkling shouts.

"I'm sorry," I mumble.

"I'm done talking about this right now," Inkling says. "But you owe me some canned pumpkin."

Maybe I Took One Tiny Bite

Nothing is different just 'cause Patne came over to my apartment. He doesn't seem to see me during lunch and spends recess playing soccer with Henry Kim and Bruno Gillicut. Gillicut used to take the best parts of my lunch every day. He hates me worse than black mamba poison but doesn't bother me anymore since Inkling bit him on the ankle.

Still, it's not like I'm going to go over and play soccer with them. Ever.

I eat with Chin and her friends Locke, Linderman, and Daley, like usual, but I don't really want to play with them in the yard. All they do right now is imagine the costumes for a musical they want to perform. It even has kissing.

I find a ball and toss it against a wall by myself.

Today, Nadia picks me up and walks me home. She's talking on and on about this new list of vocab words she's got to study for the PSAT. It is not interesting. Then we reach our corner and—

There is a food truck.

A pink food truck.

A dessert truck.

Oh no.

Let me explain about food carts and trucks in New York City. Any busy place, you see them on the corners. Usually the carts sell hot dogs or shish kebabs. In winter they have hot pretzels and chestnuts. There are candied nuts sometimes, or muffins and doughnuts in the mornings. Then there are actual trucks, bigger than the carts. They sell waffles, Thai dumplings, kimchi tacos, Indian curry, you name it.

Now we see a food truck on our corner. There has never been one there before. It's not just any food truck, either. It's a big, bright-pink truck with *Betty-Ann's*

Whoopie Pies written in large white letters on the side of it.

There is a line of people clutching money. Some of them are our regular customers. A tall white lady with wavy gray hair and a hot-pink apron is leaning halfway out the truck's window. She is wearing latex gloves and handing out whoopie pies. A young guy who looks like he might be her son wears a green apron. He works the cash register. They are wearing name tags: Betty-Ann and Billy.

Money changes hands. People unwrap their pies, which are tied up in wax paper with cute ribbons. They walk away with smiles on their faces.

I look at the menu posted on the side of the truck. Red velvet, chocolate, vanilla. The usual whoopie pie flavors. But my heart sinks when I see a sign posted at the bottom:

New!
ICE-CREAM WHOOPIE PIES
Chocolate and Pumpkin!

Nadia and I watch in shock. Kid after kid, parent after

parent—they're buying ice cream. From Betty-Ann.

Right down from our shop. Like we aren't their friendly neighborhood ice-cream store anymore.

"We should have thought of that," Nadia finally says. "Pumpkin ice cream was never going to work. What people want is pumpkin cake *sandwiching* normal ice cream."

"How could we think of it?" I say. "We're an ice-cream shop."

We walk into Big Round Pumpkin. Mom and Dad are sitting there with nothing to do. There's not a single customer inside.

After human dinner I bring Inkling a bowl of cooked kidney beans with a side of whipped cream—one of his favorite meals. We sit in my room playing Monopoly.

I have my money stacked in neat piles, but Inkling's fake cash is spread out under him, wrinkling and moving as he walks over it. He is being the race car. I am being the Scottie dog.

Spoonfuls of kidney beans disappear down his gullet every now and then.

"What are we gonna do about this Betty-Ann lady?" Inkling asks me, after buying Park Place. "What's our strategy?"

"I don't know."

"What kind of answer is that? She's taking all Mom and Dad's business! We have to do something!"

"I don't know what to do!" I snap. Because really: I just want to play Monopoly and not think about my life.

"I think you should talk to Betty-Ann. Be adorable in your Wolowitz way and get her to move the truck."

I shake my head. I am not adorable. "Mom talked to her already. "

"She did?" Inkling rustles his Monopoly money.

"Yeah. Mom said, excuse her please, but Betty-Ann was taking all Big Round Pumpkin's customers. She said, couldn't they find a peaceable solution here?"

Inkling nods and I continue: "Mom told her there were lots of places Betty-Ann could park the truck that would *support* local businesses instead of hurting them. How would Betty-Ann feel about moving to Clinton and Sackett, by the public library? Or outside the hospital's pediatric unit? Or to the new playground on Pier Six?"

Inkling huffs. "Let me guess: Betty-Ann told her to shove off."

"How did you know?"

Inkling rolls the dice and moves his race car around the Monopoly board before answering. He takes a Community Chest card and goes to jail. "I did a little spying for you," he finally says. "I know you don't like me to listen in on human conversations, but in this case I thought it was important."

"What did you do?" I move the Scottie, land on Go, and collect $200.00.

"Nothing fancy," says Inkling. "I climbed into the truck and wedged myself into a shelf. Listened in on Betty-Ann and Billy."

"What did you find out?"

"Betty-Ann says 'shove off' a lot. Whenever Billy asks a question? 'Shove off.' Like, she thinks he's supposed to already know the answer, or he shouldn't be interrupting. And when the guy from the chocolate shop on Court Street came by? You know, the dude with the extra-long scraggle beard? He tried to talk to her about ingredients, friendly and everything. 'Shove off.'"

"She sounds mean."

"And let me tell you this," says Inkling. "She's selling more pumpkin ice-cream pies than anything else. It's her most popular item."

I narrow my eyes at him. "You didn't steal one, did you?"

"Well, maybe I took a tiny bite of one," says Inkling. "Maybe I wrapped it up again perfectly so no one would notice."

"Inkling!"

"I had to taste it, Wolowitz. I had to get the full

picture of what was going on."

I sigh. "Was it any good? Could we do better at Big Round Pumpkin?"

He clucks his tongue. "I'm not one to judge. You know I don't like ice cream. And as for the pumpkin, what are you humans thinking? It was all mixed with cinnamon and spices and sugar. Sugar, when the pumpkin is naturally so sweet and delicious! I don't understand it."

"Did you find out anything else?"

"Before she came here, Betty-Ann used to park the truck by the Cranberry Street playground in Brooklyn Heights. Then the weather got cold and she decided that she could make more money moving here. Our neighborhood has a lot of schools."

"What else?"

"She makes the whoopie pies in a kitchen somewhere across the Brooklyn Bridge. Also, she's not a very nice person."

"I figured that."

Inkling rolls doubles and gets the race car out of jail. "How about we drop on her from a tree branch?" he suggests. He always thinks the laws of the outback apply in Brooklyn.

"That's not gonna help," I say.

"Yes it will."

"I'm not dropping on an old lady."

"Okay. What if we bite her on the ankle? That's worked before."

"No."

"I could haunt her food truck."

I shake my head no.

"Pop out from a rabbit warren and biff her?"

Now I don't even know what he's talking about—but it doesn't matter. "Inkling!" I shout. "I have a strategy!"

Four Fifty a Pint
Is Criminal

The next day after school, I pick up Inkling and we head over to Big Round Pumpkin. I wash my hands and pack a pint of vanilla and a pint of salted caramel, the flavor grown-ups like best. I pack them the way Mom does, decorated with a pumpkin sticker on top of each container. Then I walk out and wait on line in front of Betty-Ann's truck.

When I get to the front, I notice Billy isn't there. Betty-Ann is alone. She leans out the window, all smiles. "Hi there, handsome," she says. "What'll it be?"

"She's in a good mood," whispers Inkling, on my shoulder.

"Hi there," I say.

"Say *ma'am*," whispers Inkling. "Old people like it when you say *ma'am*."

"Hi there, ma'am," I say.

"What can I get you?" she asks.

"Nothing, ma'am. I have a gift for you from the folks over at Big Round Pumpkin," I say, pointing to the shop.

I can't believe I just said *folks*. What am I, southern?

Folks is a weird word when you write it down.

Folks.

Folks.

Folks.

If you look at it too long, it starts to seem evil. Like when you say *folks*, maybe you don't just mean "people." Maybe you're uttering an incantation that will call up an army of zombies.

Sorry. My overbusy imagination again.

Back to Betty-Ann.

"Why are you giving me a gift?" she asks, looking suspicious.

I am killing her with kindness, but I don't tell her that. Instead I say, "We think when you taste how good it is, you'll want to put our ice cream in your whoopie pies. I mean, I'm sure you're using a delicious brand already, but what we make at Big Round Pumpkin is something special. Plus, it's all organic and has local ingredients."

Betty-Ann snatches the ice cream from my hands. "How much you sell a pint for?"

"Six dollars in the shop, but four fifty wholesale, like to restaurants or food trucks who buy a lot at a time." My voice is shaky. Betty-Ann is fairly scary. "But these are a gift," I say. "We thought you'd like to try what we make. No obligation."

"Four fifty for a pint?" She pops the vanilla open and sniffs it.

"It costs a lot to make, with organic cream and stuff," I say. "But taste it."

Betty-Ann reaches for a spoon and takes a bite. For a moment, as the ice cream melts in her mouth, her sour expression turns sweet.

Is it working?

Yes! It's working.

Betty-Ann will be won over by the yumminess of our ice cream and the generosity of our gift. Her whoopie pie truck will use Dad's ice cream, and before you know it, she'll tell all her food-truck friends. The sundae trucks and cupcake trucks, maybe even the kimchi-taco and curry trucks—all of them will sell Big Round Pumpkin.

Throughout New York City, people will be eating what we make. They will be amazed at how ice cream can taste when it's made fresh and without chemicals. People will travel into Brooklyn just to try our full range of flavors. The shop will have lines out the door. We'll have money for this cool new Lego airplane I saw, and—

"Shove off, kid," barks Betty-Ann.

"Huh?"

"Shove off. You're not buying anything, so get outta the way. I got customers."

I look behind me. Sure enough, there's a line of kids in soccer shirts, fresh out of practice. They're waiting to buy whoopie pies.

"What part of 'shove off' do you not understand?" shouts Betty-Ann.

Now she is full-on scary.

I shove off.

"Four fifty a pint is criminal!" she yells at my retreating back. "I can pay three ninety-nine a *quart*. A quart!"

"Not organic!" I yell back at her as I run away. "Not local!"

"Not a *success*," Inkling says in my ear when we're safe inside my building. "I told you we should have biffed her."

It's This or Hip-Hop Dance

Saturday, Mom drags me to the pool at the gym over on Court Street—the one where Inkling sometimes swims after hours. (He says bandapats are related to the otters of the Canadian underbrushlands. Whether that's true or not, they definitely love to swim.)

At the pool, it turns out Mom has signed me up for lessons.

A thing about me is, I don't want them.

I'm not scared of the water. I just—I don't like the way swim teachers blow whistles. Or the way they sort the kids into levels.

Last time I had lessons was in second grade. I was a Neon. After Neon you move up to Cuttlefish. Then Barracuda, then Hammerhead.

To be a Cuttlefish you have to swim the length of the pool and back without ever putting your feet on the floor.

A thing about me is, I can't do that. My brain gets overbusy. I think: What if this warm steamy room was my bedroom? For a bed I could have an enormous hammock stretched out over the water. Going to sleep in it would feel like being deep in the jungle. In the morning, I could pull off my pajamas and jump straight in the water. I'd swim around instead of washing my face. Oh, but where would I brush my teeth? Not in the pool. That would be gross.

Maybe there'd be a long rack of heated towels up against one wall, and a sink—

Anyway, I'm thinking like that while I'm swimming. Before I know it, I'm standing still in the center of the lane looking at which wall would be best for the heated towel rack. The kid who's swimming behind me is crashing headfirst into my back, and the teacher is blowing her whistle.

44

"Do I have to?" I ask Mom.

"It's not a punishment, Hank. It's fun."

"Your idea of fun," I grumble. In college, Mom was a field hockey all-American.

"Sporty stuff is good for you. Team stuff."

I don't mind sporty stuff. I just can't remember the rules, and then everyone yells at me. It's the yelling part I don't like.

"I know you're not in love with soccer," Mom continues, "so I want you to try swimming. Once you finish Hammerhead, they have a team you can join."

I look up at her, pleading in my eyes.

"It's this or hip-hop dance," Mom says. "There's a boys' class starting at the studio where Nadia takes."

"Fine," I say.

"Here's the men's dressing room," Mom says. "Nadia is picking you up after class." She hands me a bag with my swimsuit, goggles, towel, cap, and lock, plus a granola bar.

Inkling is in the bag. I can tell because he weighs nearly ten pounds. I can't believe Mom didn't notice.

When I get into the locker room, it's empty, so I shake Inkling out of the towel, where he's been rolled like a burrito. "What are you doing here?" I whisper.

"I'm not gonna swim. I just want to see you in action."

"It's not entertainment. It's a class."

"I just want to see!" he insists.

I sigh as I change into my suit. I put my clothes and my bag in a locker.

I don't want Inkling to watch me in the pool. He claims to be a spectacular swimmer. Canadian otters and whatever. Also, he's battled kangaroos and evil scientists. He's traveled the world hiding in the backs of hatchbacks and the luggage compartments of trains.

Even if none of that's true, he's defended me against that dirtbug Gillicut. And against Nadia, when Halloween brought out the evil in her.

Inkling is tough.

Swim class—well, I don't expect it to be a shining moment. I don't need anyone watching me.

"Can I eat your granola bar?" Inkling wants to know. "I wouldn't ask except it's the peanut butter kind. My favorite."

"Go ahead," I say—and a plan forms in my mind. I pull my swim cap on and throw my towel over my shoulder. "It's in the locker."

I wait, watching the bag inside the locker rustle. Then I seize my moment. "Watch your tail!" I cry.

"What?"

"Watch your tail!" I say again—and slam the locker shut.

"Wolowitz!" he yells from inside. "You did this on purpose!"

"Shhhh," I say, lowering my voice to lie. "There are other people here now. You have to be quiet!"

"I'll get you for this," Inkling whispers back.

"See you after class!" I say cheerfully, clicking the lock into place.

We Look Like Defeated Supervillains

Turns out the locker room was empty because I am late. Most people are already in the pool, except a line of shivering kids waiting by lane five. A teacher in a red surf shirt barks at me: "If you know your level, go to your lane. Neons on the far end, Cuttlefish lane two, Barracudas lane three, Hammerheads lane four."

"What if I don't know?"

"Line up at lane five and we'll test you," says the guy.

Great.

Testing.

I was hoping they'd just shove me in Barracuda

without testing me. That's what level most fourth graders are.

I line up behind four other kids. We look like defeated supervillains. Colored goggles. Swim caps making us look bald. Hunched over and hugging our torsos, chilly from the shower we had to take before getting to the pool.

"Why our parents decided we should swim now that it's practically winter, I have no idea," says the girl in front of me. She is wearing a purple bathing suit and a silver swim cap with bright-green goggles. "All summer I begged to go to the pool, but did I ever go?"

I nod, but I am really looking at the kid in front of her. His brown skin and orange goggles are familiar.

Oh.

It's Patne.

And in front of him, his friend Henry Kim. Kim has a mole on one cheek, so I recognize him right away, even in black goggles and a yellow cap.

"Drat," I mutter.

"What's wrong?" asks the girl.

"I know them," I say, gesturing.

"So?"

"So."

"So what?"

"So I don't really like people I know watching me swim, okay?" I blurt. "It makes it like a performance. It makes me kick funny and then I go crooked."

"What about me?" she says.

"It's not so bad having strangers watch me swim," I explain. "They're not going to make unpleasant comments at school the next day or ask me why I kick like that."

"You're weird."

"A little, yeah." No use denying it.

The girl smirks. "No, I mean, you don't recognize me."

"I—"

I look at her. Her hair is completely covered by her silver cap. I can't see her eyes because of her green goggles. Her skin is medium color. She could be Latina or Asian American or any kind of mix. She has dimples and black nail polish and—

Oh.

It's Chin.

My actual friend. That I didn't even know I was talking to.

"You're that kid from downstairs who built the Great Wall of China from matchsticks, right?" I say, trying to make it like I knew it was her all along. "Weren't you a dead ballerina for Halloween?"

She knows I'm faking it. "You didn't recognize me in the goggles."

"More the swim cap," I confess. "Don't you think we look like defeated supervillains?"

Chin nudges Patne. "Joe, get this. Hank didn't recognize me in my swim cap."

Patne pulls his goggles up and squints at me. "Is that Hank?"

"Hey there," I mutter.

"I can't recognize *anyone*," Patne says. "Everything is blurry without my glasses, and with the caps on, we all look bald."

"For-serious, everything is blurry?" I say.

"Pretty much. For next time I'll remember Sasha has the silver cap and the green goggles, and you have blue everything," he says. "The details of your faces aren't there, but I'll know you by what color blob you are."

"I'm a blue-everything blob!" I say, laughing.

Maybe it's not so bad that Patne and Chin are

swimming with me. Even if Kim is going to take most of Patne's attention, like he always does—this could still be fun.

Then the teacher in the red surf shirt grabs my arm and points to an empty lane. "Swim here, you and the two kids behind you. We're going to do two lanes at a time so you guys don't waste your whole hour waiting for the test."

"But I—"

"Go on. Front crawl to the end, backstroke on the return."

Great.

Now I have to swim in front of everyone.

I'll Sew Up My Wounded Stomach with Yarn

When I do the backstroke, it feels like I'm in the middle of the ocean. There's nothing anywhere for miles but a few waterlogged boards from the shipwreck I was just in. I can't hear the sounds of the pool like I can with breaststroke. I can't see the bottom like I can with crawl. I can't tell where I'm going, unless I crash into the buoys on the side of the lane.

I wonder if a shipwrecked kitten is floating, all alone, on a soggy raft. He's scared of the ocean. He's mewling. I have to swim over so I can rescue him, but I can only swim on my back because of this injury I have from the shipwreck. My stomach is cut open and nearly all my insides are spilling out. I can't roll over or else my kidneys and liver and all my other guts will pour into the sea.

Backstroke, backstroke.

I'm doing quite a good backstroke for a guy whose insides are spilling out of his torso.

When I reach the kitten and save him, we'll live together on the raft. I'll sew up my wounded stomach with yarn I finger-knit from shedded cat fur. The kitten will show me how to catch fish. Together we'll survive. I'll name him Hercules.

By the time ye olde fishing boat finds us, we'll have made up a new language called Humankitty, so we can talk to each other. For example, Hercules will say, "Yao yao! Mrwwp tup tup. Prowl owl?" What he'll mean is: "No fair you ate that fish head. Can't I ever eat the head for once?"

When ye olde fisher people rescue us, I'll have forgotten how to even speak English and—

"Hank!"

What?

How do the fisher people know my name?

"Hank! Finish your lap!"

Huh?

That sounds like Chin.

Is Chin on the boat?

Oh.

Uh-oh.

I am not in the middle of the ocean speaking Humankitty.

I am in the pool. Being tested for a swim level. And failing.

I mean, I am not even swimming. I am standing in the middle of my lane, meowing.

No surprise, I am not a Barracuda. I am not even a Cuttlefish.

I am a Neon.

The same kind of Neon I was back in second grade.

I spend the rest of the swim-class hour Neoning around with a bunch of little kids.

Patne, Kim, and Chin are Hammerheads.

Maybe You Didn't Really Want to Take My Money

Aaghhhhhh!

When I let him out of the locker, Inkling does a flying pounce and bites my knee. Ow, ow, it hurts. I swat at him, but he wraps himself around my leg. Then he chews just above the knee where it tickles.

Aaghhhhhh! I stumble back and shake my leg, trying to throw him off. I lose my balance over the locker-room bench.

Crash!

I hit the floor backward, flailing my arms.

My head ends up inside a locker. My face is scraped.

Ow.

Inkling lets go.

Just my luck, it is Kim's locker. I'm lying on top of the smelly green sneakers he always wears. And the socks he's worn all day.

I feel cold seep across my back. I lift my aching head to look.

Wonderful. I tipped over an open bottle of lemonade. "Nice move, Hank," Kim says.

I try to sit up, but the angle is funny with my head in the locker. I reach out for Kim to help me, but he pulls his hand back.

"Whoops! Too slow." He laughs.

Patne is right behind him. Laughing, too. "You got new feet today?" he asks.

I would like to hit Patne right now. I would like to hit Patne, then karate-kick Kim. One of those moves where you spin around midair and the side of your foot connects—*bam!*—with the enemy's nose. Nose kick!

Only, I don't know karate. And my parents want me to be a pacifist and kill people with kindness. "Ha-ha, very funny," I say to Patne. "New feet, ha-ha."

Kim pulls a sweatshirt over his head. "You owe me a lemonade."

I sit up. "I didn't mean to spill it."

"You can buy a new one from the machine outside the locker room."

I do have a dollar, which is what the drinks in the machine cost. But I don't want to buy Kim a lemonade. It's not like I *drank* his lemonade. It's not like I even knocked it over on purpose.

Most people? If you spilled their lemonade they would say, "No problem." They would go get a towel and help you mop it up.

Not Kim.

"I don't know if I have money," I fib. "I probably don't."

"Joe can check while you go get towels," says Kim. "Joe, look in Hank's pocket to see if he has money, 'kay?"

And Patne does it. Sticks his hand in the back pocket of my jeans, which are hanging in my locker.

"Yaahhhhhhh!" Patne screams and jumps back. Shaking his hand.

"What's wrong?" asks Kim.

"Something bit me!"

"No way," I say, pushing down a smile. "What could bite you?"

"I don't know. Something." Patne's staring at his hand and squeezing it. "Wow, that really hurt."

"Nothing bit you," I say. "There's nothing there." I say it with total confidence. I even stand up, take my jeans out of the locker, and start changing into them.

I am getting to be quite a good liar. Not that it's something to be proud of.

"I don't know." Patne looks as if he might cry. "It feels like the end of my finger might come off."

"Is it bleeding?" asks Kim.

We all examine Patne's finger. It's red, but not bleeding. Inkling was careful.

"Maybe you just felt badly going into my pocket for my money," I say. "Maybe it's mental."

"Mental?" Patne asks.

"Maybe you didn't *really* want to take my money," I explain. I finish changing and sit down to put on my shoes.

"You do have money, then?" Kim says. "That's great. You can buy a new lemonade."

Oh.

Yeah.

Maybe I'm not such a good liar after all. "You can't have my money!" I yell. "Patne, I can't believe you're being such a dirtbug, to stick your hand in my pocket."

Patne looks up at me and shrugs. "Henry told me to," he says.

"You were over at my house on the weekend! You made ice cream with me. We splatted the alien poo. What kind of person splats alien poo one day and sticks a hand in a pocket another, huh? Is that a nice person? Because I don't think so."

Kim wrinkles his nose. "Alien poo?"

Patne gets very busy looking for his shoes inside his locker. "I don't know what he's talking about."

"Are you going to say something about sticking your hand in my pocket?" I ask Patne. "Are you?"

"Sheesh, Hank, you don't have to get so upset about it. We were just kidding around," says Patne.

What?

What?

"I wasn't really going to take your money."

"Oh yeah?" I say.

Patne laughs. "Of course not. What kind of guy do you think I am?"

I squint my eyes at them. "I just wanted to see if he'd do it," Kim explains, smiling. "I love seeing if I can get Joe to do stuff."

Patne socks him in the arm. "I hardly ever do stuff you tell me."

"Yes you do." Kim laughs.

"Only sometimes."

"Only a lot of times."

"Only when I want to."

"Yuh-huh."

"I wasn't really taking your money, Hank," says Patne.

"You don't need to get mad," says Kim.

I don't know what to say. I feel like an idiot. "Okay, fine," I say. "Fine."

I walk to the front of the locker room and collect some towels. Come back and wipe up the spilled lemonade in silence. Then I get my bag, hold it open for a moment while Inkling climbs in, and wave good-bye to Patne and Kim. They are throwing each other's sneakers on top of the lockers.

Laughing hysterically.

A Pygmy Hedgehog Sounds All Right

Nadia picks me up outside the gym. "Remember about pygmy hedgehogs?" she says. "Remember how you tried to convince Mom to get you one and she said no way?"

"Yeah," I say. It was a while ago, though.

"So guess what?"

"What?"

"Jacquie got two."

"For serious?"

"Yes."

"I thought you were mad at Jacquie," I say.

"I am, but she has pygmy hedgehogs."

"What does that mean?"

"It means, I don't trust her. We used to be friends, but now she's just my halfway friend. But hello? Pygmy hedgehogs!"

I laugh.

"It's worth going over there," Nadia says. "Don't you want to see them?"

"Of course. What could be better than a pygmy hedgehog?"

"Nothing!" shouts Nadia.

"Nothing!" I cry.

Inkling bops me on the ear. (He's riding on my back.) Ow!

"I mean, a pygmy hedgehog sounds all right, as far as pets go," I say, backtracking. "An invisible talking creature from the Peruvian Woods of Mystery would be much better. If such a thing existed, which it totally does not."

"Sometimes you are not a normal person, Hank," says Nadia.

"You tell me that all the time," I answer. "It's not new information."

···

Jacquie lives in a brownstone in Park Slope, which is a neighborhood a half-hour walk from our place. It's a pretty area: big town houses in rows. The wide sidewalks are lined with trees. Inkling even climbs off my back and trots alongside me for some of the walk, though on our home streets he's scared of getting stepped on.

Jacquie opens the door of her house wearing shorts and a bathing-suit top even though it's cold outside. She's got a ski hat on her head. Dance music is blasting so loud she doesn't say hi, just waves at us to come in. The hedgehogs are in a huge cage near the entrance to the backyard.

Once she turns the music down, Jacquie tells us about them. "They need lots of space," she says, "plus a plastic running wheel." There's also a litter box, tubes for them to crawl through, a couple of boxes lined with washcloths for the hedgehogs to nest in, a bowl of lettuce and another of cat food, plus a bottle of water like you'd give to a hamster.

At first I can't see the hedgies. They're hiding in the boxes. They're nocturnal, Jacquie explains, but they'll wake up if we tempt them with food.

I feel Inkling's thick furry body leaning against me as I peer into the boxes. The hedgies are so small! So spiny!

"They're babies," Jacquie tells us. "It's better to adopt them as babies because they get used to being handled."

Jacquie pulls some carrots out of her fridge and gives them to Nadia. "Put them in, and I'll tap the box gently," she says. "I think they'll wake up."

And they do! Two tiny, sleepy-eyed hedgehogs come out of the boxes, waddling toward the carrots eagerly. The darker one is Derek and the lighter one is Teakettle.

"I can't believe you named your hedgehog after Derek," laughs Nadia.

"Who's Derek?" I ask.

"Jacquie's ex-boyfriend," says Nadia. "Why would you want to remember that idiot every time you look at your hedgie?"

Jacquie shrugs. "He looks like Derek, don't you think?"

Nadia squints her eyes. "Sort of. If Derek was a hedgehog."

I swear, I will never understand girls.

Teakettle abandons his carrot midbite. He toddles

across the cage, past me to where Inkling is. His nostrils flare in and out.

He can smell Inkling!

I can't smell Inkling, but Rootbeer sure can. Other dogs can, too. Teakettle must be the same.

He comes a little closer and then starts acting strange. He sticks his tongue out and turns his tiny neck. He starts licking his quilly body, twisting into funny shapes. He's drooling all over himself.

"Your hedgie's going crazy!" Nadia says. "What's wrong with him?"

"I think he's anointing," says Jacquie.

"What's that?" I ask.

"He hasn't done it before. I only read about it."

"But what is it?"

"Something they do when they like a certain smell or taste," says Jacquie. "They twist around and cover themselves with foamy spit."

"Yuck," I say, but I laugh.

"What is he smelling that he likes?" wonders Nadia.

"Maybe the carrots?" suggests Jacquie.

"He walked away from his carrot."

"Then maybe your perfume?"

Nadia shakes her head. "He's not even looking at me. It's Derek that likes me." She reaches her hand into the cage and strokes Derek's spiny back gently.

I know what Teakettle likes, of course. Inkling. But I keep my mouth shut.

Derek toddles over and starts munching on Teakettle's abandoned carrot.

Teakettle stops anointing himself. He head-butts Derek.

Derek drops the carrot and head-butts back. They butt each other, making chirping noises. Hedgie fight!

Derek goes for the carrot again, and Teakettle hisses like an angry cat. Derek munches the carrot anyway. Teakettle lunges as much as he can on his tiny hedgie legs. Derek turns into a ball. He somehow stretches this—*floppy bit*—he stretches his floppy bit over his own back feet. Then he tucks his head in, becomes a ball, and just *rolls*.

Teakettle butts the Derek ball around the cage a bit. Derek won't unroll.

"Teakettle showed him who's boss," says Jacquie.

"Yeah. Can you imagine if you could pull a flap of

your own belly skin over your legs?" says Nadia. "So gross."

"*Ew*," says Jacquie.

"Emperor penguins do it," I say. "They have that floppy bit they use to cover the baby penguins and keep them warm. But they don't roll up in a ball or anything. They just tuck stuff in."

Derek is still rolled into a ball. Jacquie reaches in and takes Teakettle out of the cage. "You're a very important hedgehog," she lectures. "You have defended your carrot. But don't scare your friend Derek that way. It's not nice."

"He doesn't understand you," says Nadia.

"You never know," I say. "Animals might speak English."

"Yeah, right."

"Maybe they speak Yiddish and Mandarin, too," I go on. "Maybe they can write and play Monopoly. Maybe they just don't do it in front of us. Did you ever think of that?"

"Hank!" Nadia is crinkling her forehead at me.

"What?"

"We're over at Jacquie's house. Just act normal, okay?"

"Huh?"

"Normal. Pretend if you have to. Okay?"

Fine. I march over to the dining table and sit in one of the chairs there. I open my math book and don't talk to either of them.

"I already know he's not normal, Nadia," says Jacquie sweetly. "You don't have to stress."

I'm Going to Bake Her
into Submission

When Saturday rolls around again, Betty-Ann is still stealing our customers. Inkling is moping about his lack of bandapat friends. Mom is planning Thanksgiving dinner, Nadia is practicing vocab, and I am surviving fourth grade—but it isn't always pretty.

Inkling watches me in swim class. I can't stop him. He's way too smart to get caught inside my locker another time, and once I'm in the pool I have no control over what he does. I think he sits in the bleachers with the parents of the little kids.

Now, you might think your invisible bandapat

would spare your feelings when he knows you're a stupid Neon and everyone else is a Hammerhead, or because he's seen the way it is with Kim and Patne in the locker room. You might think your invisible bandapat would be all, "I have no idea why they made you be a Neon; you're a great swimmer." Or, "I've seen Henry Kim in the pool; he's not that much better than you." Something encouraging like that.

You would be wrong.

Inkling laughs and laughs. "You swim like a cat," he says, when he finally gets his breath. "You swim like a *house* cat."

We are sitting in a tree in the park across from Public School 166. After swim class, Nadia and I walked over there with Patne, Chin, Kim, and their parents. Inkling and I are on a branch in a low tree, looking down at people riding skateboards and playing on the big rock. Patne, Chin, and Kim are on the tire swing.

74

You know, the kind that has room for only three people at a time.

I don't like tire swings anyway. They make me dizzy.

"House cats don't swim," I say.

"Exactly," giggles Inkling.

"Have some sympathy."

"You should let me coach you," he says. "With my help you'd move up to Hammerhead before winter break."

"Okay, coach me." I look down at Patne, Kim, and Chin, spinning and laughing on the tire swing.

"Well," says Inkling, "you'd go a lot faster with your breaststroke if you rotated your feet like this."

"Like what?" I know he's sitting next to me, but I'm staring at empty air.

"Feel my ankles."

I pat around in the air and finally

find Inkling's ankles. They are covered in thick fur. His legs are a totally different shape than mine, and he's circling them around every which way. "I can't tell what you're doing," I say. "It seems like you're just waving them."

"I'm not just waving them. First I am rotating out slightly, at the top of the frog kick. When the legs extend, I'm flapping them in with a pushing motion. It works against the resistance of the water."

"No idea what you're talking about," I say.

"Feel my ankles!"

I feel them again. "I can't tell what you're doing," I say. "I can't see your legs."

He sighs, annoyed. "You're never getting better if you won't even try."

"I try."

"Not a lot," says Inkling. "You try, but you only try a little."

I get down from the tree and go over to the big rock. I climb to the top of it and stare at the outline of the winter trees against the sky. I don't feel like talking to anyone anyway.

• • •

"I have an idea!" Dad says, when Nadia, Inkling, and I get home. He is standing in our apartment kitchen, wearing oven mitts. His scraggle beard has custard on it, and there's pumpkin goo on his elbow. The kitchen is a mess. Flour on the floor, butter smeared on the counter, a sink full of dishes.

"What are you doing?" Nadia asks.

"I'm going to bake her into submission!" Dad cries.

"Huh?" I have no idea what he means.

"Betty-Ann. If I can make a perfect pumpkin ice-cream whoopie pie *myself*, our customers will come back. You *know* our ice cream is better. Betty-Ann will admit defeat. She'll drive that stupid pink truck back where it came from. I just have to get the hang of making the cake part," he finishes. "Here, try these."

He hands us each a pumpkin muffin. We bite in.

"Dad? These are the tiniest bit mushy in the middle." That is a nice way of saying they are totally gross.

"They're a little salty, too," Nadia confesses. "Did you use a recipe?"

"I mixed ideas from a couple recipes together," says Dad. "And made several batches. The ones in the oven have crushed pineapple, too. That seems like a cool addition, doesn't it?"

Um, no.

"What's that smell?" asks Nadia, as smoke begins to billow out of the oven.

Dad leaps forward, waving his oven mitts.

I Am Evil Because of
How Bald I Am

O ver the next ten days, Dad becomes obsessed with this idea of baking Betty-Ann into submission.

He's not really a baker, though.

I mean, he's not a baker at all.

We probably shouldn't even let him bake. Anything.

For example, he has to remember to wait till the oven is hot enough. (One batch ruined.)

And to grease the pans. (Another batch ruined.)

He has to listen out for the timer to ring, use a hot pad so he doesn't drop the pan, and not fill the tin so high the batter sloshes onto the floor of the oven.

(Ruined. Ruined. And ruined.)

Also, apparently he has to sit in front of the computer a lot, watching baking demonstration videos.

Dad buys stacks of cookbooks looking at recipes for pumpkin cakes, pumpkin cookies, and pumpkin breads. He buys muffin tins, muffin-*top* tins, madeleine pans, and finally specialized whoopie pie pans from a baking shop in Manhattan.

Since we have no oven in the ice-cream shop, he takes over the apartment kitchen, getting Nadia and Mom to work his shifts so he can perfect the pumpkin cake that will sandwich the slab of vanilla ice cream.

Some of the cakes turn soggy. Some of them crumble when they come out of the pans, and others stick. Some cakes are too crispy, some too puffy.

Some look beautiful but taste awful. Too much nutmeg or too much salt, not enough cinnamon. Inkling doesn't even like them. "I don't know why you humans don't just eat it raw," he muses. "Two slices of fresh raw pumpkin with some ice cream in between? Problem solved."

Nadia is grouchy because even though Dad pays her to work, doing all those extra shifts while he's upstairs baking means she misses art class, misses PSAT prep class, misses studying her spelling words and hanging out with Max.

Mom is grouchy because Dad is spending so much money and because sales of ice cream are way down compared to last November. "Use the public library," she says. "There's no reason you need to be buying all these cookbooks." He's paying Nadia to work extra hours, buying fancy pans, spending on cans of organic pumpkin and expensive ingredients. Most of the results end up being tossed in the garbage or given to the neighborhood shelter that takes donations of the shop's leftovers.

As if it's not enough that Dad is acting crazy and my parents are arguing—I still have to go to stupid swim class.

The other kids in Neons are babies. There I am, sitting on the edge of the pool waiting for my turn to do some doofy kickboard practice, and I'm watching Chin, Patne, and Kim learning butterfly stroke or dives.

Mom and Inkling both remind me that if I'd only concentrate harder in class, before I know it I'll be a Hammerhead. But I can't concentrate when I feel like such a loser. All of them together, and me in the baby class. My brain just won't focus on kicking or airplane arms.

It's not that Patne and Kim are mean to me, exactly. Sometimes they're funny. Sometimes they're nice. The third Saturday, we're sitting in the bleachers with Chin, waiting for lessons to start. I get the idea that we should all make up supervillain names for ourselves. "Chin, you should be The Architect of Doom," I say.

"Why?" asks Kim.

"I like building things," explains Chin. "Is that it?"

"Yeah," I say. "We built this Great Wall of China and half the Taj Mahal out of matchsticks, which was Chin's idea, even though I helped. She's always building stuff with blocks or Popsicle sticks."

"Or pipe cleaners," says Chin. She is wrapped in a towel decorated with enormous daisies.

"I think you'd have a superpower to do with buildings, like changing them all around, or putting them up instantly or something," I say.

"Completely," says Chin.

"Only evil," I add.

"Of course. Plus, I always wear a tiara."

"Whatever," I say. But hello? The whole supervillain idea comes from the way we all look in our swim caps and goggles—defeated supervillains, remember? No way is The Architect of Doom wearing a tiara. She wears Chin's silver swim cap. Also, you can't fight properly wearing a tiara, no matter what Wonder Woman thinks. I just say "Whatever," as I don't want to hurt Chin's feelings.

"What am I?" asks Patne.

I squint at him. "Lord Baldy."

He nods very seriously. "I am. You are absolutely right."

"Is that because of what he looks like in his swim cap?" says Kim.

"Yes," says Patne, still serious. "And I am evil because of how bald I am. I live in one of those big creepy mansions. I have lots of minions and a butler. I drive around in a limousine."

"You have a lot of gadgets," I tell him. "The minions make you gadgets."

"Exactly. And the limousine can go underwater if I want it to."

This is why I like Patne. When I like him. Underwater limousines are good.

"I am The Holy Terror," announces Kim.

What? I thought *I* was making these up.

"How come?" asks Patne, lifting up his goggles to look at Kim.

"That's what my mom calls me when I'm in trouble," Kim explains.

Okay. That is a good name. "Are you a religious guy or something?" I ask.

"No, I'm like a giant toddler," says Kim. "'Cause you know, that's something parents say about kids when they're rambunctious."

"A giant toddler is awesome," says Chin.

"I have temper tantrums and I always wear footie

84

pajamas," says Kim. "I have all these weapons that look like teddy bears and rattles, and I have a scream that can, I dunno . . . stop time? Yeah. I can stop time as long as I'm screaming, which is very useful in battle. But sometimes you can defeat me by giving me a lollipop."

Fine. I would have made him Kimchi, like the spicy Korean cabbage thing. He could kill people with hot pepper in their eyes and supersonic farts from eating too much cabbage. But The Holy Terror is pretty good, I guess.

"Who are you, Hank?" Chin asks me.

I have been thinking about this. "Reptiliopolus," I announce. It sounds grand and venomous.

"What?" Kim does not look properly impressed.

"I have fangs, like a poisonous reptile, and my weird scaly skin makes me angry and evil but also cool looking. I can swallow really big things, things way bigger than my head. Whole people even. And I ride around on a giant Gila monster lizard that does my bidding."

"Reptiliopolus is not a good supervillain name," says Kim. "It sounds like a city."

"It is too a good name," I say.

"Nah. How about SnakeMan?"

"No way." I am not being stupid SnakeMan.

"Or Mr. Reptile?"

"That is the dumbest thing I ever heard," I snap.

"Reptiliopolus sounds totally evil," says Chin loyally. "Don't give Hank a hard time, Henry."

"Okay, fine," says Kim. "Be Reptiliopolus if you like it so much."

She Won't Catch You.
You'll Be a Unicorn.

The next day, Dad makes six different batches of whoopie pie cakes, all of them too crunchy. Mom wraps piles of them in foil and sends me to deliver them to neighbors. I bring some to Seth Mnookin and Rootbeer across the hall. Some to Chin and her mom downstairs. Some to Mrs. Gold, the talky old lady in apartment 2E. Even to this neighbor on the third floor that I swear I've never seen before.

When I get back, Mom and Dad are having an argument. Or rather, Mom is having an argument, flailing her arms around and stomping. Dad pretty much never argues back. This time, he isn't even listening.

"You're never going to sell whoopie pie cakes to the restaurants that stock our ice cream," Mom says. "We aren't going to grow our business with cake! No one wants cake from us! We don't even have commercial ovens!"

"That Betty-Ann," Dad mutters. "Do you think she's using corn syrup? I could tell if I tasted one of her pies. Hey, do you think I could put on a disguise and buy some from her?" Then he shakes his head. "No, she'd peg me for sure."

"We should be spending our time talking to new restaurants," argues Mom. "Or seeing if Union Market wants to carry pints. Maybe some of the specialty food shops would carry them, too. We should be doing that, not worrying about the truck lady."

"Betty-Ann," Dad corrects. "Her name is Betty-Ann."

"I don't care what her name is," Mom says. "I care about finding ways to sell more ice cream this winter."

"What if I sent Hank down wearing Nadia's unicorn head?" Dad wonders.

"You're obsessed!" Mom yells. "It's driving me crazy."

"Hey, Hank," Dad says, "do you know where Nadia keeps that unicorn head she bought for Halloween?"

I do. But I tell him no way am I going to Betty-Ann's truck again after what happened when I gave her the pints.

"You'll be wearing the head," Dad says. "She'll never know it's you."

"Nuh-uh."

"Pretty please? This could be the answer, Hank. If we can uncover the secret to her ice-cream whoopie pie, we can defeat her once and for all."

"What if she catches me?"

"She won't catch you. You'll be a unicorn. Come on, Hank. You gotta help me."

Fine.

Bleh.

I get the unicorn head and put it on. It is rubbery smelling. I can only see through a small tunnel in the mouth.

This is a bad idea.

Dad is a lunatic.

I wear the unicorn head outside. A couple people stare at me as I walk up the block, but this is New York City. They see weirder things every day of the week.

I get in line and wait. Finally, I'm at the front. I try to

disguise my voice. "Four pumpkin ice-cream whoopie pies," I squeak.

"Coming up, horsie." Betty-Ann smiles.

I hand my money to Billy. "I'm not a horsie; I'm a unicorn," I explain. "I have a horn, see?"

"Sure, horsie," says Betty-Ann, giving me the pies in a brown paper sack. "You tell your Big Round daddy I said he'll never figure out my recipe, all right?"

She recognizes me! Aaghhhhh!

I sprint down the block, stumbling as I go. I screech around the corner, ripping off the head to get some air. I am certain Billy is going to tackle me from behind any minute and—

I am out of breath when I get to the park. Dad is waiting for me, sitting on a swing. "She's onto us!" I yell as I sprint up. "She knew me by my voice, or my sneakers, or something. She said you'll never figure out her recipe!"

Dad covers his face in his hands. Defeated.

I eye the edge of the park for Billy or Betty-Ann.

Nothing happens.

The silence is awkward.

"This is so embarrassing," Dad finally moans.

"You're not the one who had to wear the unicorn head," I say, sitting down on the swing next to him.

Eventually, we unwrap the whoopie pies. They're small, about the size of my palm. Each has a cute orange ribbon around it.

We are quiet as we take our first bites.

Oh.

They're good. Really good.

Well, the ice cream isn't as good as Dad's. It's thinner tasting, and the vanilla has a fake smell. But the cake part is—well, I'm so sick of pumpkin cakes, I thought I'd never eat another bite of one, but Betty-Ann's are great.

Dad chews his with a deep frown between his eyebrows. "I think it's got corn syrup," he says. "And maybe cloves?" He sniffs the cake thoughtfully. "No way are these organic."

"Dad," I say. "What if Mom's right?"

"Right? In what way could she be right?"

"What if we should just ignore Betty-Ann? And whoopie pies? What if we did concentrate on selling pints to grocery stores or getting more restaurants to use us?"

"I want people in the shop, Hank," says Dad. "We're a neighborhood ice-cream store. I don't want to spend my days packing pints for Union Market and never seeing anyone eat what I make. I want to build sundaes and watch people licking their spoons. I want to hear kids ask for double scoops. I want to give a baby a vanilla cone with fun orange sprinkles and see her face light up. Packing pints—that's not running an ice-cream shop. That's just making a product."

We head to Union Market. I watch silently while Dad spends twenty dollars on regular cloves, powdered cloves, and two big jugs of corn syrup.

The situation is getting desperate.

I Felt Like a Wonderpat

Inkling pokes me awake in the night, his claw tapping my cheek.

"Whaa?" I look over at the clock. It's three a.m.

"I threw up," he whispers.

"Huh?"

"On the floor of the bathroom."

"*Ew,*" I moan.

"And a little on the carpet in the hall," he adds.

"More *ew.*"

"Don't say *ew,*" Inkling snaps. "You wouldn't want me to say *ew* if *you* threw up."

He's right. "Sorry," I mumble.

"Try and have a little sympathy."

"Okay." I'm still half asleep. "Are you okay? Does your stomach still hurt?"

"Yes!" Inkling says, irritable. "In fact, I think I'm going to throw up again right this minute." He makes a horrible moaning noise and I hear a thump as he jumps off the bed, then a scuffle as he runs out of my bedroom. I stand and follow.

The toilet seat clonks up as I enter the bathroom. There's a puddle of orange barf seeping across the floor, and more spewing from an invisible body into the toilet bowl.

It's gross. Part of me wants to run away or call Mom—but I know I can't do either of those things. I step around the barf and sit on the edge of the tub. I feel the space over the toilet and put my hand on Inkling's furry back as he heaves.

When he's done, I pick him up and set him down on the bath mat, which is still clean. I flush and bring him a glass of water. I wipe up the barf on the floor with paper towels and spray cleaner, and try to get it off the hallway carpet, too.

"Are you sick?" I ask, when I'm done scrubbing. "Do you have a headache? A fever?"

"Nah. I'm not sick. It was indigestion."

"What did you eat?"

Inkling huffs. "What do you think I ate?"

"Pumpkin?"

"*Cooked* pumpkin. Fresh would never disagree with me. Fresh pumpkin I could eat forever and never have a moment of trouble."

"How much cooked pumpkin did you eat?"

Inkling moans. "Six cans. Well, maybe seven."

Wow. That's a lot.

I sit in silence for a moment, picturing Inkling with a can opener on the floor of our kitchen. Then I ask, "Do I need to go clean the kitchen before Dad finds a mess in the morning?"

Inkling gasps. "What? No! What kind of friend do you take me for? I wouldn't eat Dad's pumpkin! He needs that for work!"

"Whose pumpkin is it, then, if it's not Dad's?"

"Betty-Ann's."

I nearly fall over on the bathroom floor. "How did you get Betty-Ann's pumpkin?"

"I crawled into the truck and got inside a cooler. She drove across the Brooklyn Bridge to her kitchen and unloaded. Before you know it, I was inside her lair."

"Weren't you scared?"

"Bandapats are never scared. I had a strategy."

"For what?"

"Stopping her, of course."

"But—"

"No buts. When you mess with Big Round Pumpkin, you mess with Inkling."

"What did you do?" I ask.

"Well, I had big plans," Inkling answers. "I sincerely did."

"What plans?"

"Let me explain something. In the Peruvian Woods of Mystery, older bandapats punish nudnik bandapats by lurking in abandoned rabbit warrens. They *pop out* and *biff* when the little guys don't expect it. "

"Pop out and biff?"

"It's a punishment."

"For what?"

"For taking other people's pumpkins, disturbing people's sleep, maybe hogging the covers or gossiping.

For being a *nudnik*. That's Yiddish for Really Annoying Person."

"Okay, so the old bandapat does what?"

"She finds a rabbit warren, or maybe a gopher hole, and she hides. When the nudnik comes by, she pops out and biffs him on the ear."

"Biffs him."

"It's the pop-out that makes it really good, because of the surprise element. You can't just biff without a pop-out."

"So you were going to pop out and biff Betty-Ann?"

"Exactly. From inside the cooler, first thing in the morning. After that, there was no way she would keep selling her stupid whoopie pies on the same block as Big Round Pumpkin."

"But something must have gone wrong."

Inkling moans and the bath mat moves a little. "The cooler was cold. I couldn't sleep in there. I thought I'd look around for something warmer. More like a rabbit warren."

"And then?"

"I was in her kitchen, and there were cans and cans of pumpkin, Wolowitz. You can't even imagine. Way more than Dad has."

"What did you do?"

"What do you think I did?" Inkling snaps. "I figured out how to work the can opener, and I started eating. I didn't even have to chew, you know? I just opened up a can and poured that pumpkin right down my gullet until I was all swollen up."

"Gross."

Inkling sighs and crawls onto my lap. "At first, with all that vitamin A surging through me, I felt fantastic. Like a wonderpat."

"What's a wonderpat?"

"Wonderpats are bandapats who achieve greatness far beyond the everyday awesomeness of bandapats. They don't have superpowers. They just do something amazing. Like Lichtenbickle, who tamed the unicorn; or Hetsnickle, who defined the bandapat code of honor. Anyway, I felt like a wonderpat. I got really hyper. I ran around and around Betty-Ann's kitchen, just itching to biff her. I couldn't believe I had to wait probably another eight hours. Finally I decided to walk across the Brooklyn Bridge," says Inkling.

"Why?"

"It's one of those things people should do when they come to New York City, right?" he says. "And I've never done it."

"You're crazy."

Inkling moans. "The canned pumpkin was affecting me. I couldn't sit still. I felt like the bridge was calling to me. I figured to be back in plenty of time to biff Betty-Ann and make sure she never caused trouble for Big Round Pumpkin again. I found a window, pushed it open, and climbed outside."

"Then what?"

"I made it across the bridge, but when I got to Cadman Plaza, I felt queasy and threw up in a bush."

He moans again. I stroke his sticky fur.

"Then I lay underneath a park bench for ten minutes or so," he continues, "trying to work up the strength to return to Betty-Ann's. It was so depressing. Every time I sat up, there was more barf. If you don't believe me, we can go up there tomorrow. I'm sure the barf is still under this one bench, across from the library."

"That's all right," I say. "I don't need to see it."

"In the end," Inkling says, "all that energy I'd had—disappeared. I was weak. My stomach was still rumbling. I knew if I just kept going past the plaza, I'd reach Atlantic Avenue. After that it would only be a short walk to your place. So I went home in defeat. I had to crawl with my floppy bits dragging on the ground. It was pitiful."

"So you never did biff anyone?"

"No one," he says regretfully. "And I tell you, it woulda solved everything if I had."

Spot-Clean,
or the Highway

Inkling is sticky with pumpkin barf. "You need a bath," I tell him.

"No way. Just spot-clean me."

"I can't spot-clean you. I can't see where the spots are."

"I'm not going in the bathtub," he says. "Just feel around my fur, and when you hit some barf, wipe it with a paper towel."

"No way," I tell him. "You need soap and shampoo and maybe bubble bath, too."

"No way yourself," says Inkling. "It's spot-clean, or the highway."

"You can't go around smelling," I threaten. "Mom will find out about you. Rootbeer will bite you."

"Leave me alone!"

"What's the problem?" I say. "You love the water. You're related to the otters of the Canadian underbrushlands, remember?"

"Fine," Inkling grumbles. "But run the bath and then give me some privacy, okay? I am perfectly capable of using shampoo without your help, thank you very much."

I do what he says. I turn on the water and go back to bed. I'm asleep almost as soon as I lie down—but I start awake again at five a.m., because I hear the water running.

Still?

Did Inkling forget to turn it off? Did he flood the bathroom? Did he hurt himself in there and *couldn't* turn the water off because he was at death's door?

I hurl myself up and rush into the bathroom, expecting to find the floor soaked in water, an overflowing tub, and a half-dead invisible bandapat somewhere, unconscious.

Everything's fine.

The tub is full of fresh bubbles. The water is a safe

distance from the top. The bathroom is clean.

Inkling is in the tub, backstroking like an otter. A cluster of bubbles hangs off one ear. His tail is splashing gently.

What?

What?

Inkling.

He's in the tub.

I can see him.

They Only Have
Teeny-Tiny Brains

I don't need to write down the shouting and toweling and blow-drying that occurs next.

It isn't pretty.

Inkling is for-serious mad that I barged in on him in the bathroom and saw his floppy bits.

I am for-serious mad that he never told me he was visible when wet.

Inkling is for-serious mad that I won't leave the bathroom once I get in.

I am for-serious mad that he is floating around visible when Mom is going to be up any minute and coming in to take a shower.

Enough to say that we get him dry and invisible before anyone sees him, and I go off to school with Nadia.

"Jacquie's having trouble with Derek and Teakettle," Nadia tells me, as we stand on line for take-out coffee and corn muffins at the diner.

"What do you mean?"

"The pygmy hedgies keep fighting," she says. "They don't like each other."

"Why not?"

"Who knows? They're hedgehogs. We can't know what they're thinking. They only have teeny-tiny brains. But Jacquie said that hedgies sometimes don't like living with each other. They're happier alone. She should never have gotten two."

"Why *did* she get two?"

"She said two were cuter than one."

"What's she going to do?"

"She talked about bringing one of them to a shelter. Can you believe her?"

A wave of sadness washes over me. "You mean Jacquie would just, like, drop Derek off at the Animal League?"

"Not Derek. Teakettle. She likes Derek better."

"I don't care which one," I snap. "It's just so mean."

"That's Jacquie for you," says Nadia, paying for our food. "She doesn't think about others. That's why I'm only halfway friends with her now."

"Why are you even halfway friends?"

Nadia shrugs. "She's funny. Don't you have halfway friends?"

We eat our corn muffins and Nadia drinks her coffee as we walk. "Yeah," I finally say. "I do."

"Like who?"

"None of your business."

"Are they people you want to be total friends with?" she asks. "Or do you not like them enough to be total friends?"

I shrug.

"It's those guys from swimming," Nadia says with authority.

"No it isn't."

"Yes it is."

"Fine."

"So do you want to be total friends? Should Mom call their moms and ask them over?"

"Ahhhhhh!" I yell. "Mom asked you to ask me that, didn't she? You only started talking about Jacquie so you could work your way around to asking me about Kim and Patne."

Nadia looks sheepish. "You kinda busted me, yeah."

"Ahhhhhh!" I yell again.

"Mom worries about you," she says. "She thought I could talk to you better than she or Dad could, maybe."

I stamp my foot at her and make a mean face. "Is Jacquie even giving up a hedgie, or were you just making that up to get me talking to you about stuff?"

Nadia ruffles my hair and laughs. We're in front of PS 166 now. "Eat your corn muffin and go to school," she says.

"I'm dropping *you* at a shelter," I say. "You'll be in with a bunch of sad dogs and you'll be really sorry you did Mom's dirty work for her."

"Yeah, right," says Nadia.

Then she hugs me.

Ugh.

Lord Baldy Is with Us
or against Us

That afternoon, Dad picks up me and Chin from school and takes us to play on the big rock in the playground. We play alien schoolchildren for a bit, like usual, and then Chin says, "Let's play supervillains instead."

"Okay," I agree, "but is The Architect of Doom fighting Reptiliopolus, or are they teaming up to take over Manhattan?"

"Hm." She furrows her brow. Chin gives this kind of question a lot of thought. "I think we should take over all of Manhattan's *food trucks*!" she finally says. "We'll make them servants of our evil ice-cream empire."

Wow. Sometimes that girl's mind is impressive.

"We can write out the details of our evil plan," she goes on. "Then when Joe comes over, we can see if Lord Baldy is with us or against us."

"Joe is coming over?" I say. "Like, Joe Patne?"

"What other Joe is there?"

"He's coming over to your apartment?"

"Sure," says Chin. "My mom invited him and his dad to come over and stay for dinner. It's tomorrow night, I think. We're getting pizza."

"Oh."

"To be honest though," Chin continues, "I'm kind of nervous. Do you think he'll make fun of my ballerina calendar?"

"What's there to make fun of?" I lie, because that ballet calendar is really foofy.

"Or the Great Wall of China we built?" she wonders. "Or the Barbies? Or my purple bedspread? I don't want to just *let Joe Patne loose* in my room. I feel like he's the type of guy who would make critical remarks."

"Like what?"

"Like, 'Ooh, ballerina calendar.'"

"That's not critical."

"Yes it is."

"It's just 'Ooh, ballerina calendar.'"

"No," says Chin decisively. "*You* would say, 'Ooh, ballerina calendar,' and what you'd mean is 'Hey, where'd ya get that?' Or 'Do you take ballet?'"

"Right," I say. Though really, when I saw that ballerina calendar I just kept my mouth shut because, you know, if you don't have anything nice to say, don't say anything.

"Joe would mean something different," Chin explains. "What Joe would mean is: ballet is stupid."

"Yeah," I say, with a prickle of guilt.

"And Joe does this thing," she goes on, "where he acts like whatever he does is normal and whatever you do is weird. Have you noticed?"

"Oh yeah," I say. "One time I told him how I always imagine there are giant lizards lurking in the bottom of swimming pools—you know, in the deep end where the water's dark? And he acted like he'd never, ever, heard of giant lizards. Or deep ends. Or swimming pools, even."

"I always worry about sharks," says Chin.

"Exactly!" I say. "And my dad worries about piranhas. Every single person I know understands about the giant lizards, but Patne just goes 'No idea what you're talking about.'"

Chin nods and clutches my arm. "Will you come tomorrow night? For dinner?"

"Huh?"

"Come help me be friends with him," she says. "I'm sure my mom won't mind. She's just ordering pizza."

Oh.

"Joe and Henry are fun and everything," Chin goes on, "but they're just not that easy to be friends with somehow, you know?"

"I do," I say.

We are silent for a moment. Chin lowers her voice. "Will The Architect of Doom and Reptiliopolus tame Lord Baldy with the awesomeness of their Great Wall of China? Or will Lord B sneer at The Architect's ballet calendar—"

"—and mock the poor swimming skills of Reptiliopolus?" I add.

It feels weirdly good to say that out loud. *Poor swimming skills.*

Yeah, I've got poor swimming skills. It stinks.

I do wish they were better. Maybe I could actually practice or something.

But real friends don't care. Chin and I built a Great Wall of China out of matchsticks. That's what matters. Not that she's a Hammerhead and I'm a Neon.

"We will kill Lord Baldy with kindness," I tell her. "Just you watch."

They Are Pies of Evil

Next day, Patne skips after-school. We both go home with Chin. Once we're in the building, I pretend I want to drop my backpack upstairs and I go collect Inkling.

He made me promise to bring him over for dinner. Pizza is one of his favorite foods.

Chin's mom is making salads in their kitchen. We kids are supposed to go play. "Do you want to see our Great Wall of China?" I ask Patne.

"He's not interested in that," says Chin. "Let's stay in the living room."

"We built it out of matchsticks," I explain. "It took a really long time. Now we're starting on the Taj Mahal. You can send away for kits."

"Can you set it on fire?" Patne asks. "Would all the matchsticks light up, going down the length of the wall?"

"Nah," I say. "They don't have the red fire thing on the end."

"Too bad." He looks disappointed. "But yeah, I still want to see it."

"Oh, whatever. Let's not go in my room," says Chin. "Let's stay here in the living room! So much more fun."

"Fine," says Patne. "Don't show me your Wall of China if you don't want to."

"Chin!" I whisper. "We are supposed to kill him with kindness. How can we kill him with kindness if you won't let me show off the Great Wall?"

"Wolowitz!" she whispers back. "I do not want him to see my Barbies and my ballerina calendar. I thought I made that clear."

"Chin!" I whisper again. "You are not killing a guy with kindness if you don't let him in your room when he comes over."

"Wolowitz," she whispers back, "I do not even understand what killing people with kindness means."

"We agreed on it!" I whisper. "That's why I'm here."

"It sounded good at the time," she answers. "But I don't actually know what it means. Are we enemies or friends? Are we secretly luring him to an unpleasant end? Or overloading him with niceness till he falls down? Are we trying to defeat him? And is it real defeat of Patne, or supervillain defeat of Lord Baldy?"

"You are overthinking it," I whisper. "We are just being nice. We are trying to make total friends!"

"Kids?" Chin's mom interrupts us. She's standing in the doorway, with Patne's dad behind her. "Joe just came into the kitchen complaining that you two are whispering together and not including him."

"What?" I am shocked.

"Sasha, you know whispering is rude," says Chin's mom. "I shouldn't have to remind you."

Patne stares at us like what he is: a fourth grader who just tattled that we weren't letting him play. I have never seen him look like that. I didn't know he had so much as a single tattle in him.

I do feel bad we whispered. I look over at Chin, and her face is flushed pink. "Sorry," she says.

"Yeah, sorry," I mumble.

"Come see what I brought for dessert," says Patne's dad, changing the subject.

We follow him to the kitchen, but I'm not that excited to see what he brought. I am expecting a pile of strawberries at best, because Patne's dad is the kind of guy who thinks fruit is dessert. He won't even let Patne eat his Halloween

candy. But then, Chin squeals, and Patne starts jumping—and I see.

Ice-cream whoopie pies are piled high on a platter. Chocolate and pumpkin. They are unmistakably Betty-Ann's. The wax paper and ribbons give them away.

"I convinced my dad to buy some on his way here!" says Patne, still jumping. "Even though he doesn't believe in dessert!"

My face burns. My hands clench. "You what?"

Patne turns to his dad. "Can we have one each now, before dinner? They're small."

"Pretty please?" says Chin, making big eyes at the adults. "I love the pumpkin ones. It won't spoil our appetites, we promise."

"You've been eating ice-cream whoopie pies from Betty-Ann's truck?" I say, unbelieving.

"All the time," says Patne. "Or, whenever I have my allowance and my dad's not there to say no."

"Joe got me to try them after swimming last week," Chin says. "You went off somewhere with Nadia, remember?"

This is too much. "I went off to *work in my family's ice-cream shop*!" I yell. "Our ice-cream shop that's down the block from Betty-Ann's stupid truck. Why didn't you come *there*?"

"The whoopie pies are awesome," says Patne. "Have you tried them?"

"They're pies of evil!" I cry, stamping my feet.

"What?" Chin looks puzzled.

"Sometimes Hank is weird," Patne says to Chin's mom.

"Pies of evil!" I yell.

I know I am overreacting, I know. But I can't help myself. All the worry about money, Dad's crazy baking, Mom's anger, Nadia's sulking—it's been building up for ages. Here I am, killing Patne with kindness and trying to be total friends, and he goes buying whoopie pies from Betty-Ann. And getting Chin to do it, too!

A jar of Oatie Puffs on Chin's kitchen counter pops open. "Ow!" Patne rears back as if someone's hit him on the nose.

Pop out and biff!

Patne grabs his face and stumbles back. He clutches the tray of whoopie pies for support, and—

Bam! The tray doesn't just tip, it jolts into the air as Patne touches it. Whoopie pies fly across the room.

Inkling.

One pie hits Chin in the shoulder. One splats her mom's black skirt. Patne's dad has ice cream and cake crumbs in his hair. Patne, off balance from Inkling's biff, falls as whoopie pies roll under his feet. His backside thumps to the floor with a squish. Several pies burst underneath him.

"My family's shop needs you!" I yell in the mayhem. "These pies are made by a mean, not-organic lady who

doesn't care about the neighborhood. We have killed her with kindness and it didn't work. We have tried to learn her secrets and it didn't work. We have asked her to move to another corner and it didn't work. Big Round Pumpkin has hardly any customers because of her. I can't believe you're all buying ice cream at her truck when your halfway friend Hank Wolowitz has an ice-cream store right in front of your nose!"

Silence but for a few whoopie pies still rolling.

We stare at one another. Everyone is covered in cake and ice cream but me.

"What do you mean, halfway friend?" Chin finally asks. "That's not a very nice thing to say, Hank."

He's Not a Nudnik

I stomped out of Chin's apartment like an angry jerk. Now I am lying facedown on our couch. The door creaks open and shut. Inkling taps my leg.

"They're having pizza downstairs, Wolowitz. With green peppers. But I came up here to be with you."

"You biffed Patne!" I scold, pushing myself up on my elbows. "You can't go biffing people!"

"What about you? You just screamed at everybody and left without helping clean up the mess. How is that a better solution?"

"I wouldn't have needed to help clean up if you hadn't

biffed Patne and thrown whoopie pies."

Inkling clucks his tongue. "I thought you'd be grateful."

"Grateful?" I bury my face in the couch again. "Why would I be grateful?"

"You were grateful when I bit Gillicut on the ankle, back when he used to take your lunch. You were grateful when I bit Patne on the finger that time he tried to take your money. That's what I do. When the situation calls for it, Inkling takes action."

"This is not the outback!" I moan. "This is Brooklyn!"

"That Patne is a nudnik!" Inkling says. "He deserved the pop-out and biff."

"He's not a nudnik," I say, sitting up. "He's my halfway friend."

"You just screamed at him."

"I know I screamed at him, but the reason I was mad about the pies is 'cause he's supposed to be my friend."

"Really?" Inkling crawls onto the couch next to me. I try to explain.

"It's true that Patne goes off with Kim at recess and in the locker room. It's true he was a jerk about going in my pocket for my money. But I think he's funny

124

and sometimes he's nice, like when he helped clean up the pumpkin splat," I say. "And frankly, I could use a friend who isn't a girl or a bandapat. You know? Also, Reptiliopolus would never beat Lord Baldy in a supervillain battle, so instead I am trying to kill him with kindness."

There is silence. Inkling coughs. "Whatever makes you happy," he says finally. "But he seems like a nudnik to me."

I start laughing. I laugh and laugh.

It's hard to stop, and I fall off the couch.

Inkling laughs, too.

"I think you really just wanted to pop out and biff somebody," I say, lying on the floor. "After you couldn't do Betty-Ann."

He grunts.

"You had all this pop-out-and-biff energy stored up," I explain. "You had to let it out, even if it wasn't the right target."

"No way," says Inkling. But then he chuckles.

I want to go back downstairs now, but I can't figure out what to say. I should apologize for screaming at everyone and not cleaning up, I know. But I'm also glad they know about the whoopie pies of evil. Truth is, I kind of want *them* to come upstairs and tell me they're sorry they bought pies from Betty-Ann when Big Round Pumpkin needs customers.

Inkling flicks on the TV. We watch a bit of a documentary called *Snakes of Terror*. But it is nothing new to a guy who knows as much about venomous reptiles as I do, and I'm not even supposed to be home alone.

Eventually I get up. I have an idea of what I might say. "You coming?" I ask Inkling.

"Nah," he says. "I want to see what they're going to say about Peruvian snakes. I bet they don't know half of what really lives in the Woods of Mystery."

"I'll bring you a piece of pizza if there's any left over," I tell him.

I walk downstairs and knock on Chin's door. *Bam bada bam! Bam bada bam bam!* That's how I always knock, so she knows it's me. From the other side, she knocks back: *Bam bada bam bam!*

Then her dimply face is peeking out from behind the door.

"My dad is working at Big Round Pumpkin," I tell her. "You and Patne wanna go down and get free ice cream?"

It's as close as I can get to *sorry*.

"Sure," she says. And I'm pretty sure it's as close as she can get to *sorry*, too.

Fried Potato and Onion
in Your Ice Cream

When we walk into Big Round Pumpkin, who is there but Henry Kim, The Holy Terror. He's at the back table with his parents and two little sisters. They are the only customers, but they're all eating sundaes with hot fudge and butterscotch sauce, whipped cream and pistachios, so Dad looks happy.

"You all had pizza without me?" Kim says, hitting his head with his palm. "That is so unfair. You would not believe how many vegetables I had to choke down before I was allowed to come here."

He leaves his family and comes to sit with us at the

front of the store. He's full of questions for Dad. How is the ice cream stored? (There's a walk-in freezer in the back.) How did Dad learn to make it? (It was his hobby in college; he learned from a book.) How do you make hot fudge? (Long boring explanation Dad gave that I won't repeat here.)

Patne, Chin, and I order cookie-dough sundaes with fudge and pumpkin-colored sprinkles. Dad makes them. "Do you have special flavors for holidays?" Kim asks.

"Do we ever!" I say.

"But not for Thanksgiving," Dad says from behind the counter. "We'll have candy cane and eggnog for Christmas, though. I'm making them already. They go on the menu after Thanksgiving."

"What about Hanukkah?" Kim asks. "'Cause I'm Jewish."

Dad shakes his head. "No."

"Latke and applesauce!" I yell.

Patne and Kim both laugh. Chin makes a gagging noise.

"It's not going to be good," says Dad. "You don't want fried potato and onion in your ice cream. Do you, Henry?"

"No," says Kim, suddenly looking serious. "But I bet we can think of a Hanukkah flavor that *would* be good."

"Bring it on," says Dad.

"Matzo ball!" I yell. Because how awesome would that be, tiny matzo balls inside your ice cream?

"Wouldn't that be chicken-soup flavor, though?" asks Chin, sticking out her tongue.

"It could be vegetable soup," I say.

"Matzo balls are for Passover, not Hanukkah," says Kim.

Okay, fine. Not matzo ball.

"Maybe gelt?" Patne muses. "You could do something with the chocolate coins people get on Hanukkah."

Now we're getting somewhere! I get out my flavor notebook, which I tend to carry around with me now, and show it to Kim, Patne, and Chin. They lean in, looking at the pages.

They read my ideas and look at my drawings. They've got ideas of their own. Patne suggests different applesauce flavors. Kim flips back to see my Halloween ideas. Chin wants to talk about toppings and sprinkles and mix-ins.

We make notes. We make jokes. I do a couple sketches.

This killing-with-kindness thing? I think it might be working.

Next morning before school, I look for Inkling in my laundry basket. "Are you there?" I say, feeling around the clothes.

"Umumumumumum." He makes a groggy noise.

"Perfect," I say—and pour a jug of warm water over him.

Oh. Maybe I shouldn't have done that when he was in my laundry basket. Now all my dirty clothes are wet. But in my own defense, most of the time I don't know where Inkling's sitting. If he was awake, I couldn't sneak up on him with the water.

I can't write down the things Inkling says when he wakes up wet and visible. They are not polite.

Still, he's cute. His ears are huge. His tummy is round. His eyes are large and curious. It's nice to actually see him. "Everyone's eating breakfast," I say, when he stops yelling and throwing wet socks at me. "I need you to help me with something while they're busy."

"This had better be urgent," he says. "I stayed up late last night."

"It's not *exactly* urgent," I confess, "but it's fairly important."

Inkling growls. "How important? Is it going to help defeat Betty-Ann?"

I shake my head. "No."

"Will it save the bandapats from extinction and bring some of them here to Brooklyn to hang out with me?"

"No. Sorry."

"Well then, what *will* it do?" Inkling asks, irritated.

"Because those are the only things I'd really call important enough to be dousing me with water before eight o'clock in the morning."

"It'll make me a Cuttlefish," I say.

Inkling demonstrates swimming techniques on the rug in my bedroom. I lie down next to him. "Watch," he says. "You'll go a lot faster with your breaststroke if you rotate your feet like this."

I can see what he's doing, this time.

I rotate my feet.

Then he shows me how to lift my elbows in the crawl, and how to loosen my knees in the flutter kick.

I can see him.

I lift my elbows. I loosen my knees.

He shows me how to turn my head so I don't swallow water.

I turn my head.

We do these things over and over, and as Inkling demonstrates swimming, even though we're both facedown on the rug, I think about—swimming.

Just swimming. Not shipwrecks or drowning kittens or giant hammocks.

"I was head of peewee bandapat aquatics in the Norwegian deserts," Inkling brags. "I coached our team through four winning seasons."

"You did not," I say.

"I most certainly did."

I stop flutter-kicking and sit up. "Inkling! The whole point of deserts is that there's no water for peewee aquatics."

"Says you."

"Norway doesn't even *have* a desert."

A guilty look flits across Inkling's face. "Stop wasting time," he tells me. "Your flutter kick is getting better, but the frog kick still needs work. Let's see it again."

Your Predictions Are Wrong

You know how teachers want you to make predictions when you read? Halfway through every book, they make you write down what you think is going to happen.

They learn to do this at teacher school. Every teacher I've had is obsessed with it.

By now, you've probably made predictions about what happens with Big Round Pumpkin and Betty-Ann. Not because you're reading this in school; just because at this point your brain has been trained to make predictions about every book you read, unless you're homeschooled or something.

Guess what? Your predictions are wrong.

Mom doesn't convince Union Market to sell pints.

More restaurants don't begin using Big Round Pumpkin ice cream in their desserts.

Inkling doesn't pop out and biff Betty-Ann like she's nothing but a nudnik bandapat.

Dad doesn't perfect the pumpkin whoopie pie cake and win the whoopie pie war that way.

And there's not a big action sequence where I suddenly learn karate and nose-kick Betty-Ann.

So what finally happens then?

Thanksgiving comes and goes. People lose interest in pumpkin desserts.

The day after the holiday, Dad puts candy-cane and eggnog ice creams on the Big Round Pumpkin menu. Mom decorates the shop with a million recycled-paper snowflakes. And Betty-Ann starts selling red-velvet whoopie pies with bright-green ice cream.

Dad starts researching red-velvet-cake recipes.

Mom lies down with a sick headache.

One afternoon in early December, Nadia picks me up from school, stomping in her big boots. "We have to go to Jacquie's right now," she announces.

"But it's Thursday," I say. "I have work." Thursday is one of the days I clean out the recycling area at Big Round Pumpkin.

"I'll tell Mom and Dad you'll be late," she says. "This is important."

"What is?" I ask. "Why are we going all the way to Park Slope?"

"Jacquie is bringing Teakettle to the animal shelter," says Nadia, through gritted teeth. "She's doing it today." My sister is walking so fast I can hardly keep up with her.

"What can we do?"

"She said I could have him if I came home with her," Nadia says. "I told her I had to pick you up. She said hurry, because her mom would only drive to the Animal League right after school. I have to get him before she abandons him."

"What are we going to do with a pygmy hedgehog?" I ask. "Where are we going to keep it? Mom will never let us have a pet."

"I don't know what we'll do with him!" barks Nadia. "I don't have a plan. I just don't think she should dump this hedgie in a shelter. She adopted him. She promised to take care of him. He's only the size of an egg, Hank!"

I know. Poor Teakettle.

"He can ride in your tote bag," I say, patting her arm. "We can buy tissues for him to sleep on."

"Okay." Nadia nods. She is almost in tears. "I don't want to be halfway friends with Jacquie anymore," she says. "After we get this hedgie, I'm not even sitting with her at lunch. She's not a good person."

It's true, I think. Jacquie is not a good person. But I don't know how to talk to Nadia about her friends. It's always teenage stuff that is way too complicated for me to get involved in. I change the subject. "What'll we feed him?" I ask.

"Vegetables and cat food," she says. "I am pretty sure. I need to do some research."

"Okay, that's not hard; but he'll need a big cage," I say. "You can't just box hedgies up like hamsters, remember?"

"I have money saved," says Nadia. "I can buy a habitat. I worked all those extra hours while Dad was making whoopie pie cakes. I was going to save for an iPad, but that doesn't matter now. I'll buy Teakettle a place to live."

"Where will we keep him?" I wonder. "Mom will no way let us have a hedgie in the apartment. What with the seven hundred books and Dad and all."

"I know she won't," Nadia admits. "I'm, like, adopting him without a home to give him."

Then, in a flash, I have an idea.

I know what to do with Teakettle, and I know how to help Big Round Pumpkin.

Nadia and I run the rest of the way to Jacquie's.

Isn't He a Little Cute One?

Big Round Pumpkin: Ice Cream for a Happy World is now home to one of Brooklyn's only pygmy hedgehogs. Teakettle has a habitat with several levels. It's stationed by the window at the back of the shop, near a cozy seating area that's stocked with picture books and wooden blocks. Families with little kids hang out there.

Teakettle has a warm place to sleep, balls to play with, and some newspaper to scrounge around in. He seems happy there.

What's more, parents bring their children in to

see him. Nadia makes a chalkboard sign that goes on the sidewalk, telling people to come visit our hedgie. Mom puts out the word on local newsgroups and in family newsletters. Someone with a blog comes and takes Teakettle's picture. I put up flyers around the neighborhood. "Say hello to Teakettle the pygmy hedgehog at your friendly neighborhood ice-cream shop!"

It works. People come. Starting around one o'clock each day, babies waking from their naps come in to see Teakettle, read some picture books, and eat dishes of vanilla ice cream. Starting at three, kids stop in after school to see him. They buy cones. Their parents buy espresso. Pretty often they take home pints—especially the holiday flavors.

A couple days after Teakettle comes to the shop, Big Round Pumpkin starts selling its first-ever Hanukkah ice cream: geshmack doughnut. It's caramel-swirl ice cream with tiny spherical doughnuts, served with a sprinkle of cinnamon-sugar across the top of every cone.

Inkling thought of the name. *Geshmack* means "tasty" in Yiddish.

Kim thought of doughnuts. Fried foods like latkes

are traditional at Hanukkah, because of the oil. Kim told us not just latkes. Doughnuts, too.

I thought of adding the caramel swirl.

Chin thought of sprinkling the cinnamon-sugar across the top, which makes it seem more special than an ordinary ice-cream cone.

Dad found a local bakery that would make tiny organic doughnuts, and then he put it all together.

Patne helped eat several test batches and made suggestions.

Nadia wrote *Geshmack Doughnut* on the board in beautiful handwriting.

Mom didn't really do anything. But that's okay. The shop is full. It feels like a holiday in there.

On December 15, Betty-Ann and her whoopie pie truck disappear from our corner. Maybe she is defeated by the awesome power of a pygmy hedgehog and a Hanukkah ice-cream flavor. Or maybe it's just too cold to eat whoopie pies out on the street. Maybe she always shuts down once winter comes around.

I'll never know. But it doesn't matter much.

What matters is, we are selling ice cream again.

• • •

I have a new job. In addition to being in charge of recycling, I have to feed and water Teakettle every day, plus go to the store to buy his food. (Nadia has to clean out the cage. Ha!)

This means I get paid more money each week, and it also means that I can actually use my money for paying off my Lego airport, for paying Nadia back money she's loaned me, and for candy. Because you know what vegetable Teakettle gets served, but doesn't actually eat much of?

Squash.

Raw squash.

I can now stock the ice-cream-shop fridge with acorn, butternut, and delicata, as well as carrots, cucumbers, and celery for Teakettle to munch on.

He likes cucumbers best.

Inkling eats almost all the squash.

One weekend morning, I wake up and Inkling is not in my laundry basket. I feel all around the bedroom in case he's sleeping somewhere unusual. He's not there.

I get up, eat some leftover Thai food, and put on clothes. Nadia's still asleep. Mom left a note that she and Dad are down at Big Round Pumpkin, working early to fill special orders for holiday ice-cream cakes. I take my key and head to the shop. I call to my folks that I'm here, but we're not open to the public yet, so they're back in the kitchen, decorating cakes.

Sure enough, I find Inkling leaning against Teakettle's cage. I've found him here a couple times lately, after school, usually next to a pile of squash rinds.

But today, there's no squash.

Inkling pats my arm when I reach down to scratch his neck, and he accepts the waffle cone I give him— but he doesn't climb on my shoulder or say anything to me. It seems like he's busy.

Teakettle is on an upper level of his habitat, looking right at the place where Inkling is sitting. His nose is twitching. His ears are perky.

And suddenly, I get it.

Teakettle has been *listening*. To Inkling. Maybe he doesn't understand English. Or Yiddish or Mandarin. Probably he understands Inkling in some animal language shared by bandapats and hedgies, some smell-touch-grunt mix.

Inkling is teaching Teakettle what he knows. Bandapat stuff. How to drop on enemies from high branches. How to eat pumpkin without getting strings in his teeth. How to backstroke and catch Oatie Puffs in midair.

Inkling breaks off a bit of waffle cone and pokes it through to Teakettle.

Teakettle sniffs it but doesn't eat. Hedgies don't like waffle cones, apparently.

"Look at him. Isn't he a little cute one?" says Inkling, reaching in to take the bit of cone back.

As if to prove it, Teakettle rolls himself into a ball and falls over on one side.

"He really is," I say.

"He climbed under my floppy bits yesterday when it was cold in here," Inkling says. "I kept him warm!"

All that's left to tell you is that for the next two weeks, when Mom drags me to swim class, I actually think about swimming.

I rotate my feet. I lift my elbows. I loosen my knees.

I remember that Chin and I built a Great Wall of China once. And now we're building the Taj Mahal. I remember that Kim, Chin, Patne, and I invented an ice-cream flavor. Kim and I will probably never be more than halfway friends, but I remember that all four of us are supervillains scheming together to take over the food trucks of Manhattan and make them servants of our evil ice-cream empire.

I remember we can all fit on the tire swing together if we try.

When I'm swimming and my overbusy imagination wants to begin zooming around—picturing huge hammocks and drowning kittens and giant water lizards—I put it on hold. I make myself think about swimming, and all the things Inkling has been teaching me.

I didn't used to be able to do that: make myself think about swimming.

But somehow, now I can.

I rotate my feet. I lift my elbows. I loosen my knees.

Before the eight nights of Hanukkah are over, I am a Cuttlefish.

A NOTE FROM
THE AUTHOR

I realize not everyone has experienced the awesomeness that is a whoopie pie, so if you've turned back here to find out what one is, here ya go: it's a cake-and-frosting sandwich. Or cake and ice cream, if it's an ice-cream whoopie pie.

As in the other books about Wolowitz and Inkling, I am fictionalizing my favorite Brooklyn shops, parks, and restaurants. Some places I mention are real, but others are imaginary. I'm also rearranging space so my characters can get around on foot rather than by subway. The Wolowitz family lives in a combination of Park Slope, Boerum Hill, Cobble Hill, and Carroll Gardens.

Big Round Pumpkin is inspired by Blue Marble: www.bluemarbleicecream.com. Blue Marble serves pumpkin ice cream every fall, and it doesn't taste like baby food at all. Betty-Ann is entirely made-up, but I got the idea for the drama in this book from eating the wonderful pumpkin ice-cream whoopie pies at One Girl Cookies: www.onegirlcookies.com.

I would like to make a few disclaimers here. First, Hank is not a reliable reporter. I doubt it's really true about that black mamba eating a parrot, and other things Hank says about snakes are not exactly facts. Second, Inkling is a big liar, and nothing he says about geography or anything else should be taken as true. Third, there's a heck of a lot to read if you want to safely rear hedgehogs. I did some research, but then I adapted what I learned about them to suit my fictional purposes.

Kim gets his name from a young friend of mine. His uncle won an auction for the chance to have his nephew's name in my books, and HK was nice enough to say it was okay if his namesake was badly behaved.

Thanks always to Bob for support, and gratitude to

Apte for the joke about creamed herring. A big debt and a large bowl of geshmack doughnut to Bray, Kaplan, Siniscalchi, Sun, Polster, Sarver, Gamarra, Mlynowski, Aukin & Aukin & Aukin, and Bliss.

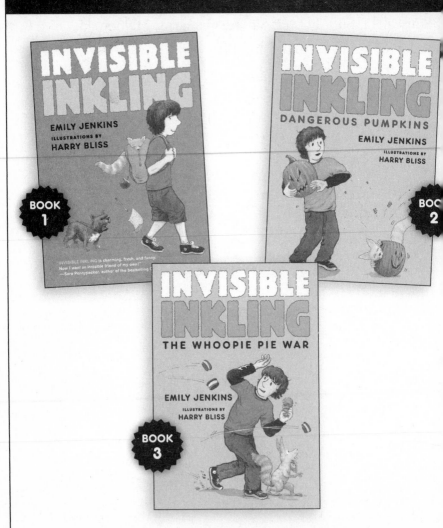